MW00882457

May you fulfi[ll] purposes & pla[ns] for your life. Know t... LOVES & CARES for you, wan[ts] the very BEST for you. He has crea[ted] you special and unique to do what only you can do. So, TRUST & OBEY Him fully. Then DREAM BIG !!! and watch to see how God brings each of the dreams He has placed within you to pass.

Much Love,
Carlessa
&
Sephina

# THE SEPHINA SERIES

(fictional depiction based on Genesis 30, 35, 37, 39-50 in the Bible)

# JAH

## "His Name Is the LORD!"

(Psalms 68:4 King James Version)

## CARLESSA F. WILLIAMS

WESTBOW
PRESS®
A DIVISION OF THOMAS NELSON
& ZONDERVAN

Copyright © 2018 Carlessa F. Williams.

All rights reserved. No part of this book may be used or reproduced by
any means, graphic, electronic, or mechanical, including photocopying,
recording, taping or by any information storage retrieval system
without the written permission of the author except in the case of
brief quotations embodied in critical articles and reviews.

Holy Bible, New International Version®, NIV® Copyright ©1973, 1978, 1984,
2011 by Biblica, Inc.® Used by permission. All rights reserved worldwide.

Scripture taken from the King James Version of the Bible.

This is a work of fiction. All of the characters, names, incidents,
organizations, and dialogue in this novel are either the products
of the author's imagination or are used fictitiously.

WestBow Press books may be ordered through booksellers or by contacting:

WestBow Press
A Division of Thomas Nelson & Zondervan
1663 Liberty Drive
Bloomington, IN 47403
www.westbowpress.com
1 (866) 928-1240

Because of the dynamic nature of the Internet, any web addresses or
links contained in this book may have changed since publication and
may no longer be valid. The views expressed in this work are solely those
of the author and do not necessarily reflect the views of the publisher,
and the publisher hereby disclaims any responsibility for them.

Cover Design by Tabatha J. Williams.
Chapter intro illustrations by Alfrena Moosa and Tabatha J. Williams.

ISBN: 978-1-9736-1340-4 (sc)
ISBN: 978-1-9736-1341-1 (hc)
ISBN: 978-1-9736-1339-8 (e)

Library of Congress Control Number: 2018900038

Print information available on the last page.

WestBow Press rev. date: 1/26/2018

# CONTENTS

# DEDICATIONS

This book is first dedicated to an Awesome God, Jah, for His Love, Goodness, and Faithfulness to my family and me. He is credited for giving me the creative idea for and inspirations while writing this, The Sephina Series.

Second, I dedicate this book to all its readers, young, mature, and the young at heart. May you find at least one thing that will bring a bit of love, hope, enlightenment, or even laughter to your life and heart.

Yet the ultimate dedication of this book goes to all the youth of this time period, the year 2018 and beyond. Young people, you are not only the world's future leaders, but you are also today's influencers. May this book encourage you to make the right choices beyond your feelings and beyond your circumstances, and to seek wise counsel. There are absolutes and absolute truths. May you have a desire for and live the Ultimate Blessing: seek, find, and develop trustworthy beliefs, relationships, and attitudes; take on the challenges of life, seeing them as opportunities for growth; and fulfill the purpose and plan you were created for. You are precious to the One who created you, and you will never be abandoned or forgotten when your trust is in Him. Give Jah first place in your life. He will not fail you.

Always let His love and truth be your guides!

Special love and dedication to my many young nieces, nephews, godchildren, cousins, family, friends, and neighbors.

There is a God who created you, and He loves you!

# SEPHINA

*I*t is a time long-ago, in a faraway land. Here lives a beautiful Nubian maiden named Sephina. She is the eleventh of her father's twelve daughters. However, she is hated by her older sisters, because their father favors Sephina above them all.

Sephina's father, Jacobee, is a very wealthy man in their land, called Bronaeh. He has had four wives, but Sephina's mother was the love of her father's heart. They were married a long time, but Sephina's mother, Chanelle, was barren. As they got older, her parents cried out to their God, Jah, to give them a baby. Jah granted them their desire—a beautiful daughter they named Sephina. For this reason, Sephina is her father's precious princess.

Because Jacobee is now older and somewhat wiser, he takes the time to teach his young princess about Jah and His goodness. Jacobee has experienced numerous injustices during his lifetime, however, Jah has provided, protected, and always come to his aid. Jacobee recognizes too how some of those injustices were direct results of his own foolish choices, wrong attitudes, actions, or reactions. These are some of the reasons he desires to impart to Sephina what he has learned. Oh, how he wishes he had done the same for his older children. Now it somehow seems too late for that. Yet he continues to try, although his wisdom seems to fall on deaf ears. Therefore, Jacobee finds occasion to sit with Sephina and share his words for living, often within earshot of her siblings.

At a very early age, about four years old, Sephina accepted her parents' God, Jah, as her own. Sephina's father taught her, as did his father and his father's father, that Jah is love, and that Jah is always good. During one such occasion, as Sephina's older sisters were tending the sheep in the field, Jacobee took Sephina to the pastures where they camped. As he and Sephina walked toward the camp, Jacobee had one of his talks with her. Sephina, now five years old, listened intently to her father's words.

Jacobee stopped suddenly, causing her to stop as well. Jacobee turned and then looked down directly at Sephina, as he told her, "Jah's love for you is even greater than my love for you, Sephina."

Her heart jumped with excitement as she heard his words. She held them to be the greatest thing her father ever told her about Jah.

Sephina knew that her father loved her. So she reasoned that Jah must truly love her.

That night, as they sat around the fire with all the older sisters, Jacobee continued his talk and explained how Jah is the One True and Living God. He also told them,

"Jah is much greater and more powerful than the evil one—Jah is ever-present, knowing all, and seeing all. Your initial wrongdoing takes you down a path that separates you from a relationship with Jah. You then become more and more easily influenced by the evil one. But once you accept Jah as your God, you become His child, not just His creation. You can trust Him with your lives—to provide for and to protect you. Jah is even quick to forgive us when we do wrong, if we would only ask Him."

Sephina was thirteen years old when her mother gave birth to her little sister, Jasmine. But Chanelle died shortly after the baby was born. This greatly saddened the family but especially Sephina and her father. Still, Sephina was a loving child, filled with kindhearted compassion for others, excitement for life, and a sense of adventure. Sensing and knowing of Jah's love for her comforted Sephina's heart after her mother's death.

The names and ages of Sephina's older sisters at the time Jasmine was born are: Ruby (26), Simone (25), LeVette (24), Danielle (24), Judith (23), Natalie (22), Gabriella (21), Ashley (20), Isabel (19), and Zebeulah (18). Sephina has only one brother, Dinnie (15), who is also her closest friend.

It is Sephina's older sisters who usually take care of their father's sheep. Occasionally she has opportunities to work with them. But usually their father sends Sephina to check on how her sisters are doing. Several of her sisters feel that Sephina only spies on them and then reports back to Jacobee their wrongdoings.

Most of Sephina's sisters dislike her because of the special attention Jacobee pours upon her. Just a year earlier, he gave Sephina a special coat designed with many beautiful colors. This gift is true evidence that their father favors Sephina above them all. But it's Sephina's dreams that make them hate her even more. Sephina has big dreams for her future. Sometimes these dreams get her into trouble.

Just a year later, when Sephina was about fourteen years old, she went to check on her sisters. As was her custom, she proudly donned her beautifully colored coat. Her warm, dark brown complexion brought the already vibrant colors of her coat to life, and her stride seemed majestic, confident, and carefree. Even so, she had to trek up and over the steep and rocky hill that divides her village from a small forest that opens to the neighboring lush pasture, not far from their home. Sephina normally accompanied her father on such a journey, but now that she was older, Jacobee had begun allowing her to take such ventures as did not exceed a daylong round trip.

During this visit, Sephina excitedly shared with her sisters another of her dreams. Most of the other dreams she shared were simple and easy to figure out, and some of them even came to be. As the youngest and smallest maiden for most of her life, Sephina thought that sharing her dreams provided her a way to be heard and not always overlooked and rejected by her older sisters. However, this dream she believed was special—actually a sign from Jah. Surely, they would be as excited about her special dream from Jah as she was ... right?

"Sisters! Jah has given me a special dream. I don't understand it yet, but I believe it is a sign from Him."

She continued and told them how in her dream, they each bound a bundle of wheat. Then each of their bundles of wheat bowed before her bundle of wheat. After Sephina shared her special dream with her sisters, they simply laughed at her, shoved her, and ridiculed her so that she ran home crying.

While running, Sephina slipped and fell. She tried to get up but realized she had badly injured her ankle. She tried crawling, but the rocks made it very difficult. Sephina knew that it would be unlikely for anyone to come looking for her anytime soon. Her father would think she was with her sisters, and her sisters—well, they wouldn't care if she made it home safely or not.

Sephina knew that she needed to get home before it got dark and before any wild animal came across her path. She prayed and asked, "Jah, please help me!"

She tried walking, only to fall again, this time sliding down a small slope. Sephina faintly cried out, knowing the unlikelihood of anyone hearing, but she trusted Jah.

"Help! Help me, please!"

As if in direct answer from Jah, a young man, about nineteen years of age, came to her rescue. He was tall and rather muscular; his hazel eyes were accented by his sun-darkened skin of a golden-brown complexion; and he had a face that was pleasant to look upon, which often radiated a bright and gentle smile; yet his lower face and cheeks were now covered with short, shadowy newly grown whiskers.

Sephina, both surprised and excited, smiled and anxiously told him, "Thank you, thank you so very much!"

He smiled as he knelt at her side and offered his assistance. "My name is Cooran. How can I help you, little one?"

Sephina said, "I'm really glad to meet you, Cooran," but quickly let him know that she was not so little. As she explained her situation, the strong young man easily lifted her small-framed body and proceeded to take her home. Cooran looked around at the rocky and seemingly remote terrain, and then asked, puzzled, "Where do you live, 'Little One'?"

Then he chuckled as she quickly corrected him by telling him, "I am Sephina of Bronaeh."

"And where do you live, Sephina of Bronaeh?" Cooran asked with a big grin.

As Sephina pointed the way home and he started walking in that direction, Cooran then asked her, "What are you doing out here all alone, Sephina?

She began to tell Cooran of her recent encounter with her older sisters. Sephina was so thankful to both Jah and to Cooran for his finding her and saving her life.

Once with Sephina's family, Cooran explained how he was on a long journey, traveling to his home country. Sephina told Cooran about Jah and how he could trust Jah to protect him on his journey. Cooran and Sephina quickly became good friends before he continued his journey home. Before leaving, Cooran advised Sephina to be wiser in her dealings with her sisters.

As Sephina grows in her relationship with Jah and desires to follow and obey Him, she learns more about Him as she spends time in prayer–talking with Him. She discovers that Jah's love for her is unconditional, meaning that His love for her continues even when she messes up—like the times she has not obeyed her parents or when she does not want to forgive her sisters.

Now Sephina is fifteen years old, and Jasmine is almost three. Sephina's older sisters are going on a long journey to take the flock of sheep to a distant pasture. Sephina hoped that she would be able to join her sisters and show them that she was mature and able to help them in the fields. She believes that by helping with the sheep, she will gain her sisters' love and acceptance. But her father tells Sephina she must stay back to watch Jasmine, while the elder women of the home tend to other tasks. He notices her unusual reaction of reluctant obedience to his instructions. Even though she obediently stays home, she also shows impatience in her care of Jasmine and a sulky attitude towards the elder women.

Later that evening, Jacobee calls Sephina to come and sit with him outside, under the starry skies. She approaches him with a sluggish walk, limp shoulders, and downcast eyes. Jasmine has already fallen off to sleep, and Sephina is free from her responsibilities of the day.

As she sits across from her father, Jacobee asks, "Sephina, why the long face all day?"

She shrugs her shoulders, pouting.

Jacobee continues, "I know you were disappointed that you could not join your older sisters, but you were needed here."

Sephina starts to say something but changes her mind. She wants to ask why Dinnie could not have watched Jasmine instead, but she knows Dinnie is responsible to help their father with heavier tasks when and wherever needed.

Jacobee tells her, "As you already know, we don't always get to do what we want. It's more a matter of doing what is needed. I know this would have been your first opportunity to take a long journey with your sisters. However disappointing as it was for you to stay back to attend to Jasmine, I have never seen you react this way. Tell me, what's going on with you, Sephina?"

She sits silent for a moment, still pouting. Then she says, "Father, I just wanted to prove to my sisters that I could be helpful to them with the sheep. Instead, I had to stay and play with Jasmine. Father, I am no longer a little girl and can really help with the sheep."

Intentionally, she says nothing to him about gaining her sisters' love and acceptance. Sephina feels her father has not acknowledged or is simply unaware of her sisters' disdainful feelings toward her.

"That is all fine, Sephina, but we needed you here instead to care for Jasmine. Isn't she more important than some flock of sheep?"

He continues, "You are usually so good at caring for and spending time with Jasmine; however, today you were short and rough with her. Your mothers told me how you were rude and disrespectful to them as well."

He then asks her, "Sephina, do you believe that Jah is pleased with your actions and attitude today?"

As Jacobee looks at Sephina, he sees her angry face become wet with shameful tears as he continues, "I know that I am not pleased, for you have hurt many people today. And that alone hurts Jah. Understand also that reluctant obedience can be just as damaging as outright disobedience."

Sephina immediately gets up and hugs her father, asking, "Father, please forgive me! I deeply apologize for my behavior today." She then asks, "Do you think Jah could forgive me?"

Jacobee quickly tells her, holding her face between his hands and looking into her eyes, "I forgive you, and Jah is a greater Father than I am. So I know He will be even quicker to forgive you once you ask Him." He smiles as he hugs Sephina, with tears now filling his eyes.

Sephina then runs into their home, finds each of the elder women, and asks their forgiveness. Afterwards, she goes to kiss the sleeping Jasmine and promises herself to talk to Jasmine in the morning.

Before retiring to bed, she goes out to the open skies once again—this time to talk with her heavenly Father, Jah. With a heavy heart, she tells Him, "Jah, please forgive me for my unkind attitude and actions toward my family and You, causing much hurt. My heart aches for allowing my disappointment to cause me to drown out Your voice and instead listen to the evil one."

As her heart lifts with the joy of His forgiveness, Sephina continues her talk with Jah. "Thank You so much for Your love and forgiveness. Please help me so that my attitudes and actions bring only glory and joy to You and never again hurt and disappointment."

She smiles as she says, "Good night, Jah! I love You!"

Though she always tries, that will not be the last time Sephina is disobedient, makes a wrong choice, or has a poor attitude. However, she has learned that after such actions, her heart aches until she asks Jah to forgive her and to help her do what is right. Each time, He forgives her. She always tries to make such actions fewer and farther between. In any case, Jah promises to be with her always. With her trust in Him, Sephina takes on the challenges of life without complaint. She is energized by Jah's goodness and faithfulness towards her.

The following day, to Sephina's delight and surprise, she is to accompany her father. Of course, she wears her beautiful coat of many colors. It is a full day's journey to the fields where her older sisters are tending the sheep.

That night Jacobee and his daughters stay in the fields under the open heavens. Sephina enjoys being outdoors on nights like this. A gentle spring breeze rustles the leaves of the few trees nearby, spreading the fragrance of the bush jasmine. The moon illumines the skies and everything around them, revealing the vastness of the valley where they are encamped, the rocky hills nearby, and the mountains in the distance, and the stars dot the heavens. They hear an occasional bleating as the great number of sheep settle down after their full two days of roaming the rough terrain in search of this wonderful stretch of lush, green pastures.

Once the sheep have settled, Jacobee and his daughters sit around a crackling fire as they eat and talk. Having her father present, Sephina is emboldened to share a second recent dream she believes is another sign from Jah. This dream reveals how the sun, the moon, and eleven stars showed reverence to her. Sephina still does not know what her dreams mean, but she is certain that Jah has a special purpose in her future to fulfill. If only her sisters could see that she is worth loving.

Even so, after she relates this second special dream, her sisters become very angry with her. Natalie and several others jump up, furious, and walk away, their faces twisted with disgust.

Zebeulah loudly questions her, "Sephina, do you plan to one-day rule over us?"

Others shout at her, asking, "Who do you think you are?"

Sephina's sisters think of her as foolish and spoiled by their father's special affection. After hearing this dream, even her father rebukes and questions Sephina about her thoughts of her family bowing before her.

"Sephina, what is this dream of yours? Do you expect to one-day rule over me, your mothers, and your brother and sisters?"

Sephina is too hurt and embarrassed to respond to her father. She thinks that if anyone would understand her heart and her dreams, it would be her father. And yet he does not. She is heartbroken and feels misunderstood.

Her greatest desire is to obey Jah and to fulfill His plan for her life. Though still rather young, Sephina has learned that each person must continuously choose to obey Jah or more easily fall under the influence of the evil one. The evil one can only deceive people to think wrong thoughts, to speak evil words, and to do bad deeds. Sephina remembers her own experience of falling under the evil one's influence, just the day before. The evil one desires only to steal, kill, and destroy humankind. Sephina has tried to share with her sisters what she has come to learn and understand, but they want to hear nothing from her—not her good deeds advice and definitely not these dreams of hers.

That night, Sephina feels a chill of rejection from her family that she has never experienced before. However, as she looks to the heavens with tear-filled eyes, she feels the warmth of Jah's love cover her as she turns on her side and drifts off to sleep.

Now, a few years later, Sephina a young woman of seventeen years, again in her beautifully colored coat, comes to check on her sisters. In the passing years, she has tried to be humble yet wise in her dealings with her sisters, knowing their dislike for her. She has long since stopped sharing any of her dreams with them. Still, she has no idea what her two special dreams from Jah might mean.

However, the day before taking on this assignment from her father to check on her sisters, Sephina finally built her courage. She asked her father for some private time alone with him. That evening, she and Jacobee sat around a camp fire outside in the fresh air and starry skies. He asked her, "My daughter, what is on your mind? Do you have another dream you want to share?"

Sephina smiled a bit awkwardly, "No, Father, no more dreams." She paused and then said, "I would like you to hear me out on a troubling matter."

Jacobee's eyebrow rose, and he asked her, "Oh, what is troubling you, my precious daughter?"

"*That* is part of the problem, Father!" she replied.

Jacobee looked at his daughter quizzically and asked, "What do you mean?"

She told him, "Now that I am older, I've realized something disturbing. Father, you have shown much favor to me that you never extend to my siblings. For all the years I can remember, you have done this. And it is not fair to them, and it is not fair to me."

Jacobee quietly listened.

Sephina continued, "Father, do you realize that you are short and impatient with all my older siblings—even Dinnie, who is always there for you. You have an issue with Ruby, refusing to forgive her, and you continuously blame her no matter who is at fault; you—"

Then Jacobee anxiously interrupted her. "Sephina, you talk in this manner to your father?"

She told him gently as she touched his hand, "Father, I mean no disrespect, but you're usually not very kind to my sisters. And they blame me. They long to sense your love, yet you constantly find fault with them. Father, I appreciate the love you shower on me, but that should be shared with all your children. Still you put me above them—belittling them. For this, they want nothing to do with me, and who could blame them?"

Then with tears in her eyes, she said, "And I foolishly told them of my dreams, which only hurt them more. For this, I am truly remorseful, and I will apologize to them."

Finally, Jacobee took Sephina's hand into his own and said, "Daughter, you are right. Jah has warned me of my wrong dealings with them. But they don't seem to listen to me or to Jah's instructions."

"Father, just begin to show them some kindness and a little love," she told him with a smile. "And Jah will work on their hearts towards Him. Just trust Jah as you've taught me to do."

She kissed Jacobee on the forehead and thanked him for hearing her out. Then she said to him, "Good night, Father, I love you."

Finally finding her sisters, Sephina is grateful after searching for almost a week. Thankfully, two days earlier, a stranger was able to direct her, since her sisters had moved quite far from their usual grazing pastures. Sephina is happy to see her sisters and their large flock, for she is rather tired, and her food supply has run out.

She also excitedly anticipates that her apologies to her sisters will prompt their forgiveness and the start of a fresh, new relationship. She knows it will take some time—more so with certain sisters than with others—but she hopes for a better future with them, especially with her father's promise to do his part.

However, when her sisters see her in the distance, Isabel vehemently announces to the others, with hatred in her voice, "Here comes that dreamer in her royal robe."

As the others look, some of her sisters then agree, "Let's kill Sephina and throw her into the pit."

Natalie sarcastically comments, "I wonder what will become of her dreams then?"

Ruby overhears their plan and said, "Let's not kill her but only throw her into that abandoned well behind the big rock. She will not be able to get out, yet no blood will be on our hands."

The sisters all agree to let Sephina rot away in the dried-out and abandoned well. Ruby, however, secretly plans to later rescue her from the pit and send her back to their father. In the meantime, she needs to leave the camp to find some vines and cloth that she can weave together for a rope to rescue Sephina.

When Sephina arrives at their camp and before she even greets them, her sisters grab hold of her and strip her of her beautiful coat. She is horrified by her sisters' cruel treatment. She has always known that they dislike her, but now, she can see hatred in their eyes. Sephina cries out to them for mercy and tries to apologize, as they throw her into the pit.

"Sisters, please don't do this. Have mercy on me, please!"

Her sisters only laugh as Simone gives her the final push into the pit. The bottom, slightly muddy, softens Sephina's landing. As she sits at the bottom of that pit, feeling distraught, she prays to Jah for His mercies and help. He reminds her of the special dreams He has given her and His promise to always be with her. She determines to hold on to her dreams, as Jah also promises that He will one day fulfill them. Though she still does not know what her dreams mean, they give her hope that she has a future and that she will somehow escape rotting in this abandoned pit.

Even so, her heart aches because of the hatred she saw in her sisters' eyes towards her, now evident from their treatment. So again, she cries out to her sisters for mercy, until finally she sees them looking in to measure the amount of rope they need to lift her out. Her heart is encouraged. She joyously thinks, *Jah has softened their hearts.*

She recalls the words of her friend Cooran. In the years since their encounter, she has tried to deal more wisely with her sisters. But no matter what she says or does, it only angers them more. Her very presence seems to upset them.

"What could I do differently or where can I go?" she constantly asks herself.

She eventually has come to realize that she can only love them, despite their dislike for her, and forgive their mean attitude toward her. Now she must love them despite their hatred toward her and forgive their physical cruelty.

Unknown to Sephina, as several of the sisters sat to eat bread, they saw a group of travelers coming toward their camp. Judith had a discussion with some of her sisters. They decided to make a profit by selling Sephina rather than killing her. They reasoned that besides keeping their hands free from her blood, after all, she was indeed their sister.

So once her sisters pull Sephina up from the pit, to her own shock and horror, they immediately sell her to the passing merchants, even as she begs them not to. Now Sephina's hopes at being freed from the pit are dashed by her sisters' betrayal of actually selling her into slavery.

Not much later, Ruby secretly returns with her ropes, intended to pull Sephina from the pit. But when she arrives to rescue her, Sephina is nowhere to be found. Ruby confronts her sisters and says, "Sephina is not in the pit. Where can I go to hide from Father?"

Being the oldest, Ruby knows that their father will hold her responsible, as he does for everything else that goes wrong. Her sisters tell her what they've done and how they kept Sephina's coat. They then collaborate and agree to tell their father that some wild beast probably killed Sephina, since they found only her torn coat while returning home.

When they tell Jacobee their story and give him Sephina's torn coat, he cries out with a loud voice. Looking at the torn coat, he mourns for his precious princess, Sephina, and no one can comfort him. From this day forward, he begins to keep Jasmine closer to himself, now that she is the only child of his beloved wife, Chanelle.

T he travelers take Sephina to a land far away from her home. The journey is long, hard, and dusty, taking several weeks. Her hands are bound in front of her by a rope that extends several feet and is attached to one of the many oxen, which carry all sorts of treasures. These treasures include spices, incenses, and nuts; rich and colorful cloths; goblets of gold, silver, and earthenware; and various crafts and exotic merchandise. There are six other people tied as she is, also to be sold as slaves. The caravan is rather large, with camels carrying the massive amounts of food and water supplies for the journey.

They travel for close to a month, making a number of stops for trading along the way, before reaching the desert. As they turn a bend around a large mountain, the narrow path they follow opens to a vast sandy expanse. In the far distance stands a grand structure, shining magnificently as the sunrays reflect off its golden domes. They are still some distance away. Soon afterward, they settle down for the night. It takes a full day and most of the following day before they enter this great kingdom.

As they enter the city gates, a massive palace is revealed in the background, topped by those golden domes. Shortly after the caravan arrives and secures a designated place to conduct business, the residents from this city flock around to view, touch, sample, and finally purchase the various goods. Soon Sephina is handed over to her new masters, an official of that land and his wife.

The official is this kingdom's captain of the guard. His name is Paninear, and his wife is called Delfar. Sephina is given the name Myra. She first works in their fields planting and then harvesting crops of grain. She is in awe of the beautiful, lush, green, and colorful fields of various grains and produce found in this kingdom. Never has she seen such splendid grazing meadows and livestock all around her.

Sephina notices how life here is greatly enhanced in having access to the great river that flows throughout this land. Another thing she enjoys in this foreign land is the annual festival which celebrates the memory of the king's oldest son, Cooran, who died at a young age. Just hearing the name brings fond memories of her friend Cooran from years past. Sephina lets this celebration remind her to think of home and to pray for her family and her friend, Cooran.

Because of Sephina, Jah causes the fields of her masters to prosper and grow, and they notice. Just after her fourth year in the fields, Sephina is promoted to work in Paninear's house. She is so faithful and efficient in her duties that the mistress of the house compliments her as being an excellent worker. Delfar expresses her trust in Sephina and gives her full authority to care for the household and all other affairs as well. Sephina stays in favor with the mistress of the house for more than three years, until something disturbing happens.

Not only is Sephina excellent in her work, but she is young, strong, kind and graceful, and extremely intelligent. She also has a shapely form and a face that is exceptionally beautiful to look upon. The master of the house begins to turn his attentions more and more toward Sephina. Delfar notices and becomes very jealous.

One day, Sephina goes to the market for her mistress. As she is returning, someone grabs her from behind, and she screams for help. As she struggles and turns, she realizes it is her master. Suddenly, someone takes Paninear by the neck from behind. This causes her attacker to release her. It is the blacksmith Norac who comes to her rescue, fighting off her attacker. He tells her to run, and run she does, as fast as she could.

Then Sephina realizes that she is running to the house of her attacker, the master. What can she do? Sephina prays as she continues toward the master's house.

"Jah, You are my loving Father. Thank You so much for Your continuous guidance and protection. Right now, I am running to the house of my master, for I have nowhere else to go. Please, protect me from his evil plan. Thank You, Jah! For I trust You with my life."

Paninear has previously threatened to take Sephina away to

another province to make her his new wife. And she wants no part of that life.

When the master later returns home, he and his wife argue late into the night. After Sephina's return from the market out of breath, then later whispers from and chats with neighbors, Delfar figures out what has taken place. On the next day, as Sephina is doing her chores, she hears a noisy commotion. As she looks up, there are two guards coming toward her. Delfar has called the guards of the kingdom and told them to throw Sephina into prison, accusing her of stealing.

While Sephina is in prison, she decides to use her own name rather than carry the slave name, Myra, given to her by her previous owners. Somehow, she feels she has gained a bit of freedom, yet she is given the most grueling tasks she has ever known. At night, she is in the lowest part of the dungeon, where the ground is cold and damp, but the air is thick and putrid, barely breathable in the darkness. During the day, Sephina, with many other female prisoners, climb steep and uneven steps to an upper level, five floors above. There they walk by twos, down a drafty tunnel with a few torches alternating on both walls, barely lighting their path.

After they have walked several miles, the tunnel opens into a large cavern that is lit by many torches and a bit of sunlight streaming through from the farther side. There, the female prisoners meet and work with the male prisoners, cutting, carrying, or pushing heavy stones used to build the palaces and royal homes for those governing this land. Though it is grueling to work with these heavy rocks and stones, Sephina takes opportunities for this specific task, in order to get closer to real sunlight and fresher air. The food is a mushy slop but filling; the water is gritty but refreshingly cool in the heat of the long, hard, and dusty days of work.

Rather than complain, Sephina just works even harder and thanks Jah for His protection. She trusts Jah even now and knows that He is with her. Soon Jah gives her favor with the prison's supervisor, and he puts Sephina in charge of all the women prisoners. Even in prison, Sephina recognizes Jah's great mercies toward her. She sings to Jah, praising Him, proclaiming that His mercies endure forever and telling Him how truly thankful she is to Him for His faithfulness.

One day two of the prisoners, who once served in the king's palace, are very sad. Sephina inquires of their reason for being sad. Each of them has had a dream the night before, a dream she does not understand. Sephina tells them of her God, Jah, and how He can give them the meaning of their dreams.

These former servants of the king are amazed, along with many of the other fellow prisoners, at Sephina's talk of a God who is personable—hearing, even listening, and, actually answering the prayers of His subjects. They express having no such relations with any of their many gods—which they fear and try to avoid—except for the terror of their gods' displeasure and demands for sacrifices.

Gladly, the two prisoners are anxious to tell Sephina what they dreamed in order to hear what Sephina's God will tell them. So Sephina asks Jah to reveal to her the meaning of their dreams, and He does.

The first prisoner was once the king's chief cupbearer. She dreamed of seeing three branches of a ripened cluster of grapes on a vine. Having the king's cup in hand, she squeezed them and served the cup to the king. After hearing the first prisoner's dream, Sephina tells her, "In three days, you will return to serve again in the king's palace. When you do, please don't forget me here in prison. For I have been wrongly accused and was forcefully taken from my homeland."

The cupbearer is overjoyed at the news and embraces Sephina. Now she only has three days to wait and see how trustworthy Sephina's interpretation of her dream will be. Sephina smiles with hope and then turns to listen to the dream of the king's other servant.

The second prisoner was formerly the king's chief baker. Because of the interpretation of the cupbearer's dream, she is extremely excited to tell her own dream as well. She tells Sephina how she dreamed of carrying three baskets of bread and baked goods on her head, which the birds came and ate from.

Sephina then somberly tells the second prisoner, "Also in three days, you—" She pauses with a heavy heart but then continues, "you will not return to the king's palace, but instead, you will die by hanging."

This prisoner rejects Sephina and her interpretation, cursing Sephina's God. Over the coming days, Sephina tries to speak to this prisoner, to encourage her to receive Jah's love for her and to ask Him to forgive her for any wrong she has done. With anger and bitterness, this prisoner wants no part of Sephina's God. Sephina prays for her still.

On the night before the day of truth, the former chief baker privately speaks with Sephina. With a heavy heart, she confesses her wrongdoings in the courts of the king and asks Sephina if her God could possibly forgive her for such acts. Sephina reassures her that if she asks Jah, He will gladly forgive her. She reassures the servant that no wrong is too great for Jah to forgive. The servant prays to Jah and receives His forgiveness. Despite knowing her fate, still the former chief baker awakens the next morning with a smile on her face, accepting joyfully the freedom she has found in Jah.

Exactly three days after Sephina interpreted the two dreams, which happens to be the king's birthday celebration, each of the two prisoners' fates unfolds exactly as Sephina said. Unfortunately, the first prisoner does forget her, and she remains in prison. Sephina sighs deeply, realizing that she was forgotten. She had hoped that Jah would somehow use the cupbearer to find an opportunity to ask the king to pardon her and release her from prison. However, she rejoices, knowing the freedom the chief baker has found in Jah.

Though disappointed, Sephina trusts Jah still and proclaims Jah as a faithful God. In deep thoughts, Sephina is reminded of her own dreams of many years ago and is encouraged. Though Jah still has not yet revealed to her the meaning of her own dreams, strange as they were, Sephina knows in her heart that Jah has some great plan for her.

Time goes by and life for Sephina continues in the bowels of the king's dungeon. Sephina is diligent with whatever task is before her, and she continues her daily encouragement to the women prisoners. She motivates some to trust in and to follow Jah. A good number have done so, even influencing some of the male prisoners to ask Jah for forgiveness for the wrong acts that caused them to be there in the prison.

Of course, a great number have rejected her, her God, and the message of Jah's goodness and faithfulness. Others scorn her, asking her, "If your Jah is so good and faithful, why are you still stuck in this dungeon?"

Sometimes she finds that question haunting her, yet she finds strength and encouragement from her own dreams as Jah's promise to her. She is able to tell them boldly and with a smile, "Even though it seems that Jah has forsaken me, I trust His promises to me. And one day, you will witness His faithfulness for yourselves."

Some ponder the idea, but many ridicule and reject her seemingly foolish talks. Then, exactly two years later, to the day of the fulfillment of her interpreted dreams unfolding for the king's two servants, something out of the ordinary happens. It has been noised abroad several days earlier, even down in the dungeons, that the king is angry and will not be celebrating his birthday this year. In fact, he is ready to execute a number of his officials.

Very early, on the morning of the king's birthday, which usually even the prisoners get to celebrate, several guards come with haste and much commotion into the depths of the dungeon. When they arrive at the women's prison, Sephina is caught off guard, talking with some of the women prisoners and giving thanks to Jah for another beautiful day. The guards abruptly take Sephina away, and as they do, some speculate that this is Jah's promise coming to pass, while others laugh, saying that it is her day of doom.

Sephina is eventually told that she is to stand before the king. She has no idea what this could possibly mean. For a brief moment, she thinks of the chief cupbearer, wondering whether at last she has been remembered and is being freed to return home. She prays to Jah for His guidance and wisdom to fulfill His purpose, whatever the reason for the king's summons.

Because of the king's urgency, Sephina is hastily cleaned up, though not properly dressed, to be presented before the king. Once she is escorted before the throne of the king, as instructed, she keeps her head bowed low and her eyes cast down. She is brought before the king's throne by guards to her left and to her right.

She stands gazing steadily downward. Then finally, the king speaks. He seems rather agitated, and his voice sounds unnaturally raspy and tired. At length he says to Sephina, "I have been told that you are able to understand dreams and to interpret them. Is that so?"

She bows before responding and lifts her head as she was instructed. Before her sits a man, who seems tormented. He looks wild, with bloodshot eyes and dark circles indicating the loss of proper rest. She responds: "Yes, mighty King. My God, Jah, has given me the ability to interpret dreams."

The king hesitates, and then he roughly asks, "Your God is Jah?"

Sephina quickly answers, "Yes, your Majesty. Jah is a good and wise God."

Then the king harshly states, "I do not know nor do I serve this god of yours. Who is this Jah?"

"Jah is Creator of all things good," Sephina quickly, firmly, and gently responds, "and He knows and loves all of His Creation— which includes you, O King." She continues, "Only through Him am I able to interpret dreams."

With that, the king makes a grunting noise and ponders for a second. He softens and states, "I have two dreams, and I have no understanding of either one. Not even my wise men or magicians are able to explain them. So perhaps your Jah can give you their meaning."

"Please, O King," she answers, "do tell me your dreams."

The exhausted king then begins to anxiously but carefully tell Sephina his two dreams. Immediately she tells the king what his dreams mean. She continues by giving the reason why they were given to him by Jah.

She tells the king, "The two dreams have the same meaning. But because of the urgency of their message, two dreams were given to you, O King."

The king is first relieved, as he feels a peace come over him. He is very impressed by this maiden's ability to tell him the meaning of his dreams. He is especially amazed, since neither his own magicians nor his wise men had anything at all to offer him regarding his dreams. He turns to ask them, "Do you have knowledge of any such events ever taking place?"

The wise men and magicians talk among themselves and come up with the simple answer to the king, still aware of the threat of execution. The chief of the wise men humbly says, "No, your Majesty!"

The king breathes deeply, feeling much more relaxed and more like himself again. He then tells them, "You wise men, quickly, take the magicians with you, and search the ancient scrolls and records to help solidify or refute this maiden's predictions. Return to me with your findings."

After they have left the chamber, the king smiles as he says to Sephina, "I find clarity in your interpretation, and I am most appreciative of your ability to give me understanding of my dreams."

Sephina quickly reminds the king that her ability is a gift from Jah, the God whom she serves. She then explains to him that Jah has given him these dreams as a warning of a devastating plan, orchestrated by the evil one. She adds excitedly that Jah has also provided a plan to counter the evil one's plan.

Then, with sober urgency she tells him, "Jah's plan will prove critical to your future survival and that of your people and keep your realm, O King, from death and destruction."

Just then, the wise men and magicians return, reporting that nothing was found either to help or to discredit Sephina's interpretation. Only time will tell. The king states as much and then politely asks, "Young maiden, what is your name?"

She tells him, "I am Sephina of Bronaeh, your Majesty," and then bows.

The king smiles and says, "Sephina, I trust your predictions are true, but only time can prove their validity. Please tell us of Jah's plan, so we can save our kingdom."

Sephina shares Jah's plan with the king and his audience. She then gives praise to Jah for His goodness and His wisdom. The king is relieved from his feelings of torment and frustration and thankful to this new God, who is looking out for him and his kingdom. For this reason, the king loudly proclaims in agreement with Sephina, that indeed,

***"Jah is both Good and Wise."***

# THE SECRET PRINCE

*I*t is a long-ago time, in a faraway land. Here lives a mighty but kind king called Rohaan. His kingdom, Daaveran, is grand in size and wealth. He and his people are celebrating the birth of his firstborn, a son he names Cooran. Then word comes that his beloved wife and queen, Madeline, has died shortly after giving birth. The king and his people are greatly saddened, for she was both a loving wife and a gentle queen.

After almost a year of mourning, King Rohaan takes the counsel of his advisers to choose a wife. In strengthening relations with a neighboring nation, he receives one of their royal maidens, Velmon, as his queen. Unbeknownst to the king, she eventually proves herself to be evil—so evil that her jealousy turns into hatred for the future heir to the king's throne, Cooran. Before the lad reaches his fourth birthday, Queen Velmon secretly orders the child to be killed. This takes place at a time when King Rohaan attends his duties in territories of distant regions under his rule. Queen Velmon secretly gives this harsh and disturbing order to one of her trusted servants, to kill the lad and bring his burned remains to her.

Upon King Rohaan's return, he is told that Cooran fell very ill and died. Queen Velmon tells him that Cooran's body had to be burned to keep the sickness from spreading to others. She cries as she gives the king the ashes of Cooran's remains. Cooran was his life, his only connection to his loving wife, Queen Madeline—the joy of the king's heart. The king cannot be comforted for many years. Even so, Queen Velmon promises King Rohaan to one day soon give him an heir to his throne. As many years pass, Queen Velmon is unable to produce the king an heir.

However, instead of killing the child as he is ordered, the

queen's trusted servant gives Queen Velmon the ashes of a lamb about the size of the lad after secretly entrusting the prince to an older, childless, but loving couple, Salamo and his wife, Merta. He tells them of the queen's wishes and charges them to take Cooran far, far away. The servant emphasizes that the lad's identity not be revealed until it is safe. The servant provides a way out of the kingdom for the couple and the child, giving what he is able, including several treasures for the child. He gives them things Queen Velmon instructed him to destroy as well, like Cooran's mother's ring and his birth certificate. The ring can be sold to help with daily living necessities for the couple and the child. And the certificate is to be given to the prince when he is older and better able to make wise decisions. The older couple love Cooran and raise him as their own. For his safety, they call him Norac.

Many years later, on Merta's deathbed, she convinces her husband to reveal to the prince, now fifteen years old, his true identity. Before she dies, she and her husband remind him of his real name, Cooran, which sounds familiar to him. Then they present him with the ring that belonged to his mother and a royally stamped certificate of his birth. Cooran is initially shocked by this new revelation. However, he is more concerned about letting his adoptive parents, especially his mother, know how much he loves them and appreciates their love and kindness to him throughout the years. Cooran stays with his mother, holding her hand until she has taken her last breath.

After Cooran and his father bury his mother, life continues, except for the great void now left in their lives. Salamo tells him more about the wicked Queen Velmon and Daaveran, the country in which he was born. There has been no news about that kingdom over the years. Yet Salamo explains that they journeyed very far from Cooran's birthplace to assure his safety. They moved several times, going further and further north each time. Salamo tells Cooran that he is free to venture to the land of his birth but cautions that he needs to be wise in doing so. He prepares Cooran as best he can for his eventual journey home, telling him of the obvious and unseen dangers to be aware of.

Salamo mentions to Cooran how he greatly resembles his father, King Rohaan, in looks and stature.

"But your eyes," he tells Cooran, "are like those of your birth mother, the warm and loving Queen Madeline."

Salamo knows this because, as he told Cooran, he and his wife once worked in the palace serving Queen Madeline. Though all this news is new and exciting, although sad, Cooran vows that his place is there with his adoptive father. So they live, love, and comfort each other.

Salamo lives only three years after the passing of his wife Merta, and then Cooran is left on his own. Having nothing left to keep him in the only country he has known, Cooran packs up all that he has and sets out for the greatest adventure of his life. He has grown to be a strong but gentle young man. During his journey, he happens across travelers that he may join, if they invite him and seem safe. He sometimes stops in villages and towns to work for shelter and meals.

Although Cooran misses both his adoptive parents, he finds this journey to be quite the adventure. However, he sometimes feels their presence, believing he hears their voices guiding or even warning him. He is experiencing new foods, meeting people from diverse nations, and even exercising some of that wisdom Salamo taught him. Cooran is now encountering and having to distinguish more between those with genuinely good intentions, those with crafty, evil plans, and all others in between for his own survival. He is thankful for the talks his adopted father shared with him to help him face such life challenges. Even when Cooran was a small lad, Salamo began teaching him some nonaggressive maneuvers and then, as he got older, some protective fighting techniques, which have all come in handy.

Now Cooran's adventure has brought him to mountains so tall, he cannot climb them; many others, though a lot smaller, he has no choice but to climb. However, his second favorite of all his adventures is experiencing the great seas. He actually hears the sounds of crashing waves hitting the rocks even before he sees the great waters. Cooran has never seen so much water in one place. The waters extend far beyond where his eyes can see.

Cooran accompanies a small caravan that venture to the seas as part of their annual ritual. He gets to feel the wet sands squish between his toes before the cold water covers his feet. The water is crystal clear and feels immensely refreshing. He walks just a little deeper and cups his hands to gather and drink from this great lake. Before he can, someone warns him to only dip his tongue before drinking. Thankfully he does, for he immediately releases the remaining waters from his cupped hands. To his amazement, this great body of water is refreshing to the touch but not for drinking. Everyone has a good laugh.

Cooran is warned also not to go too deep, for the waters have the strength to drag him under and further into the deep. He adheres and stays close enough to the edge to enjoy the coolness of the water on his feet, without the danger of being carried away. Even there he encounters new and different creatures, like the starfish beached along the shore; seashells of different colors, shapes, and sizes, some rough and hard and others smooth and fragile; and even sea birds. In a nearby fish market he sees numerous fish and sea creatures he has never seen before. What an amazing experience!

Yet Cooran's favorite adventure begins many months into his journey. One day as he is walking alone in an open, rocky, and seemingly untouched territory, he comes to a stop, thinking he has heard a cry. He listens intently and hears the cry again.

"Help!" To his surprise, he hears a young maiden cry out. "Help me, please!" Cooran follows the cry and comes upon a young maiden of fourteen years. She has fallen on the rocks and slid down a small incline. Cooran runs to her side and asks, "How can I help you, little one?"

"I'm not so little," the young maiden says, wiping her tear-stained face, "but I did hurt my ankle. I tried walking, but it really hurts."

"By the way, my name is Cooran." He feels safe and comfortable to introduce himself by his given name for the first time during his journey. He decides to use only the name Norac for the rest of his journey. He lifts and carries her up the small slope and then looks all around. Puzzled, he asks her, "Where do you live, little one?"

She says, "My name is Sephina, and I am not—"

Cooran interrupts her with a chuckle. "I know, I know, you're not so little. Okay, Sephina, where do you live?'

She thanks him for rescuing her and then points the way to her home. She smiles as she expresses how appreciative she is to meet him. At first, Cooran still doesn't see any evidence of a town or village. As he walks, he finds that they are on a hill and the village is just below them.

He then asks the maiden, "What are you doing out here all alone, Sephina?"

She sighs. "I was just returning from my sisters, who are tending our father's sheep. My father sent me to see how they were doing."

"That was nice. How are they?" Cooran asks.

"They are fine. But it wasn't so nice," Sephina admits. "My sisters don't like me very much."

She goes on to explain that she told her sisters of a dream she'd had which suggested that they would one day bow before her. "They became very angry, pushing me and screaming and laughing at me. So I started to run home. That's when I fell."

"Are you a princess, Sephina?" Cooran asks with a smile. "I noticed your beautiful coat."

"No," she replies with a shy smile, "my father just treats me like one. He is the one that gave me this beautiful coat."

Finally, they reach Sephina's village, and several people are now running towards them.

"Please, Cooran, don't tell my father about my sisters," she begs him.

"I won't repeat a word," he assures her, smiling.

Sephina's father and other family members come with worried faces to greet them. Cooran introduces himself and allows Sephina to tell her story. They thank and welcome Cooran as they take Sephina to tend to her ankle. Jacobee, the maiden's father, is especially grateful to Cooran. He knows the danger of wild beasts finding Sephina as easy prey, had Cooran not found her.

Cooran stays for several weeks, helping in the village and tending the sheep in the fields. He works hard, yet he enjoys his encounter with Sephina's large family. Never has he known someone with so many siblings. And for all Sephina's sisters, she has only one brother, Dinnie, who seems to be Sephina's closest friend and protector. Cooran eventually meets Sephina's ten older sisters, in the course of helping with the sheep. He also has opportunities to play with her younger sister, Jasmine, while in the village. Sephina's family takes very good care of Cooran and don't want him to leave.

Cooran considers returning to this land if things don't work out for him in the land of his birth, despite the noise and clatter of so many women. Having a family again, even though this one is much larger than what he is accustomed to, really feels good.

During this encounter, Cooran has become rather fond of Sephina—his "little one," as he likes to tease her. *What a delight she is,* he thinks. He thinks Sephina to be rather wise for her age, despite sharing her dream with her older sisters. Cooran smiles at the thought.

By the time Cooran is about to leave, Sephina is back on both feet. However, during his stay, they have become very good friends. Sephina has joyfully told Cooran about her God, Jah, and how good and wise He is. She also tells him, "You can trust Jah with your life, and He will keep you safe on your journey."

Before leaving, Cooran encourages her, "Sephina, be wise in your dealings with your sisters."

She smiles and thanks him again for rescuing her.

Cooran has enjoyed his stay with the family of many daughters and has quickly bonded with the single son of that clan. There is never a dull moment among them. He has even learned some valuable life lessons during his stay with Sephina and her family.

Cooran now cherishes his new knowledge about a God that loves him and is always near, looking out for his good. He learned the name of this God, Jah, and Jah is said to be the One true and living God. His parents spoke of and reverenced such a God, but they never mentioned His name. Cooran is pleased to have learned that he can even talk with Jah and know that He listens and hears.

Cooran journeys on refreshed, with his bundle filled with breads, treats, and his water supply. He continues to make short stops here and there, replenishing and adding what he can for the still long journey ahead. He even has occasions to test Jah's protection. On one such occasion, for miles and miles around him, there is nothing but desert sand. He has walked for many hours and not seen a single person near enough to greet. He is tired and needs to rest a while. The sun is directly overhead, and he somehow has grown disoriented. As he spins around looking, he is not sure which way to go. He then says, "Okay, Jah, I am now lost. Can You direct me in the way I should go?"

Cooran continues to look around him, with nothing but a featureless horizon in every direction and only the hot, beaming sun above. Then, as he looks again, in the distance something is stirring. His first thought is of horses galloping toward him, creating a large, thick dust cloud. As it approaches, it seems the sun is beginning to disappear as the dust cloud widens and the wind begins to blow. Cooran then realizes that a massive sandstorm is heading his way. Where can he run to protect himself? There is nothing in sight as far as he can see. Cooran runs as fast as he can, covering his face with the large head cloth he uses for protection from the sun's rays and for such times as this.

He then cries out, "Jah, I need your help. Please protect me."

The first band of sand begins to hit him as the winds begin to push him around. Cooran stumbles, covering his face and protecting his eyes and nose from the elements. Then the wind whistles as it strengthens, tossing him around, and the sand blows thicker, making him unable to see anything. He somehow loses his footing and then falls, tumbling down a mound of sorts. As he gathers himself, he takes to crawling and feeling his way, continuing to ask Jah for His protection. Cooran suddenly gets a strange feeling of peace and thanks Jah for his safety.

As he continues to crawl, his hand touches what seems to be a stone. He blindly crawls, feeling the stone's expanse. The more he crawls in that direction, the taller the stone grows. Soon it blocks him from the blasts of wind-driven sand. Even the whistling sounds subside. Cooran can now uncover his face and eyes, and he sees that he has crawled into the opening of a very small cave. It is just large enough to cover and shield him from the elements. He moves in a little closer after surveying his surroundings. He detects no scorpions, no snakes, no spiders, or any other creepy crawlers. He is aware of such dangers and has even sighted a few during his journey. But thankfully, he's had no such encounters.

Cooran shakes the sand from his clothing and his bundle. He decides to get something to eat and drink as he waits for the storm to pass over. After eating, collecting his belongings, and checking his surroundings once again for any unwanted critters, he rests against the stone wall, letting the strong whistling of the winds nearby lull him to sleep. Cooran sleeps until the silence awakens him. The sandstorm has finally passed, having lasted about two hours.

He sees the sun beaming just outside the cave. He gathers his bundle and crawls from the opening of the cave. Outside, he stands up, stretches, looks around, and gives Jah thanks for His protection. Then, looking up at the sun, he is better able to determine the direction in which he is to travel.

Now refreshed, Cooran estimates that he is about ten days from his destination. After walking for several miles, he encounters a man who did not survive the sandstorm. All but one clenching hand is covered by the sand. Cooran has no tools for a proper burial, so he can only move on. Before doing so, he does cover the exposed hand with sand and finds several stones to place over the covered body. His heart aches for the loss of a life, and again he thanks Jah for protecting him from a similar fate.

As he walks further, Cooran happens upon a small pouch that seems to have been uncovered by the sandstorm, or maybe the dying man had been holding it before his demise. To his great surprise, it holds several gold and silver coins. Later, Cooran is rather appreciative for that same pouch. Several days after, Jah protects him when he encounters a group of bandits heading in the opposite direction. He is somehow able to convince and appease the bandits with coins from the pouch he found.

Finally, Cooran is himself rescued after he has run out of supplies, just a day or two away from entering the kingdom of his birth. As he comes around a bend and glimpses the large golden domes of the city in the far distance, his empty stomach growls. He has no food and less than enough water to last him another day. As he hastens toward the city, he realizes that it is not as close as he had thought. In fact, the kingdom is still more than a day's journey away. Again, Cooran asks Jah to help him make it to the land of his birth.

As the hot sun begins to set in the western skies, Cooran stops, looks to the heavens, and thanks Jah for his last drink of water. The water refreshes him and gives him a burst of energy that lasts a few more hours, as he continues toward the great city before him. As he stops to rest for the night, without food and now without water, he acknowledges his peace and trust that Jah is still looking out for him.

Cooran falls asleep for several hours but is suddenly awakened by noises coming from behind him. A small caravan is headed his way in the deep twilight. He gets up and waits until they are upon him. They stop and share food and drink with him, which he gladly accepts. As they settle there with him for the night, Cooran tells the travelers of his journey and his thankfulness for their help. The leader invites him—Norac—to join them for the remainder of the journey. Cooran gladly accepts and then offers the leader the last silver coin from the pouch. But the leader refuses to take it, telling him with a big smile, "You will one day need it more than I. Save it as my wedding gift to you."

Cooran reluctantly puts the coin away. He thanks the man, pondering what he said. Then he smiles and joyously thanks Jah for saving his life once again.

That very night, Cooran reflects over his whole life's journey and the numerous times he has encountered Jah's protection over him, just as his "little one," Sephina, had said. A day and a half later, along with the small caravan, Cooran finally comes upon Daaveran, the kingdom he was told is the land of his birth. He once again embraces the leader and thanks everyone for their kindness towards him. Having much daylight still, the caravan goes straight to market to sell and trade their wares. Then Cooran breathes a thankful prayer, as he takes in the sights and sounds of his new home.

Cooran enters the magnificent gates of this kingdom and breathes deeply. He thanks Jah for His faithfulness to bring him through these gates alive and walking strong. As he enters, a group of the largest golden domes he first saw several days ago are in front of him yet some distance away from the gate. He learned this is the palace of the great king of this kingdom, his father. Stately green palm trees line the path to the entrance of the palace gates and its outer courts.

Immediately inside the kingdom's gates are marketplaces on either side. Deeper into the city are the homes and businesses of the citizens of this land. Many people are walking about, travelers with camels being loaded and unloaded, and soldiers either riding horses, walking, or simply standing guard.

In the distance he sees numerous fields of colorful grains and produce. A great river flows through this kingdom as well, with livestock drinking and grazing in the fields. This is an amazing kingdom, a refreshing welcome from the dusty desert he has just left. Cooran takes in the beautiful scenery and then begins to search for a starting place for his new life in this kingdom.

Earlier, during his travels, Cooran decided that his appearance should be a matter of concern. He is not sure if he will be recognized, since he has no idea how his father may now look. For this reason, he has not shaven the hair from his face, which he grew throughout the latter part of his journey. Nor has he cut his hair, making his appearance unlike those of the men of the land. He decides to use the name Norac until he finds it safe to reveal who he really is.

As he searches for work and shelter, he comes across Jacq, the kingdom's blacksmith. Jacq has a son, Nan, who is about the same age as Cooran. Cooran introduces himself and asks, "I am Norac. Can you use another strong worker?"

Jacq sees Cooran's muscular form and quickly answers, "Food and shelter until you prove yourself. There is lots of work now, with the king's new horse-driven chariots." Cooran gladly accepts Jacq's offer.

Nan and Norac quickly become best friends. As time goes on, their friendship grows strong enough that Cooran trusts Nan to share his secret. Cooran is relieved to finally have someone he can confide in. Nan keeps Cooran's secret until the very day that Cooran reveals his identity.

With time, Cooran learns that the evil Queen Velmon is still alive and well. She never gave birth to an heir to the king's throne and has become more hateful and bitter. The king has children with his concubine, yet celebrates the birthday of his 'dead' son, Cooran, every year in his memory. At first, Cooran is content with his life as Norac. This is true, especially after several years of working for Jacq, he is given the chance to see his father regularly.

As Jacq is growing older, he begins to give more of the heavy lifting to the younger men, relying more on Nan and Norac with the business. Jacq has come to trust Norac and considers him as his own son. Cooran has worked hard and proven his worth. Though fascinated with the new chariots, Nan prefers working with the common folks and their wooden carts and is happy to have Norac deal with the royals and their grand chariots. Although Jacq, Nan, and Norac all worked together to build these chariots of metal, Norac is given the job to maintain the king's chariots. Even so, a longing to personally interact with his father—to talk with him, get to know him, and express love to his father—starts to become unbearable.

Now Cooran is twenty-seven years of age, and not only does his heart long to know his father, but he has also seen a beautiful maiden that he wants to pursue. This maiden seems to stand out from most of the maidens in this kingdom. Her complexion is darker and her form, though relatively short in stature, is very becoming. He has seen her quite often in the marketplace but only from a distance, and he does not know who she is.

Cooran is utterly surprised to discover that this maiden is the slave of an officer of the king, who is actually captain of the guard. Cooran is not sure if this is a good thing or not. This information does not diminish his attraction to her, but rather makes her more appealing. Despite her position as a slave, she walks with an air of confidence and a smile that radiates joy. As he inquires further, he learns that she is called Myra.

Cooran has saved up most of his coins, including his one silver coin, since working for Jacq these many years. But to purchase the freedom of a slave will require much more. Cooran thinks and quickly decides that Jah will provide a way for him to marry this maiden, if it be His will. He then smiles at the thought. Cooran realizes how much he has come to seek guidance and trust his life to Jah. He thanks Jah for his encounter with his wise "little one" who joyfully told him of Jah's goodness and love.

One early evening as he is leaving work, Cooran sees the beautiful maiden, Myra, again in the distance. He has decided to finally go speak with her, when suddenly a man forcefully grabs her from behind. She cries out, and he instinctively runs to her aid. As he fights with the man, he tells the maiden to run, and she does.

The man calls out, and several guards come to his aid. Soon Cooran learns that the man is Paninear, the captain of the guards and the maiden's master. Paninear then orders his guards, "Take him and throw him into prison," as he brushes himself off.

Nan happens across the guards as they are taking Cooran away. "Tell Jacq to help me," Cooran shouts to Nan.

Soon Cooran has been in prison for almost a month and Jacq has not been able to get him released. Nan has taken Norac's place caring for the king's chariots. Then one day the king finally asks Nan, "Where is Norac? Is he ill?" Nan explains that Norac has been imprisoned.

Then Nan adds, "O King Rohaan, my father, Jacq, would like an audience with the king." The king agrees to meet with him, and Jacq asks the king for a pardon for Norac.

Instead, the king orders, "Have Norac brought to my courts at once."

The king has noticed the care Norac takes in his work. Secretly, the king has come to feel a special fondness for this young blacksmith. There is something about Norac that makes the king think of his beloved first queen, Madeline. It is Norac's eyes. Not only is the color similar, but his eyes possess a soft gentleness as well.

When Norac arrives, the king says, "Tell me your story, Norac." And Cooran does.

The king then said with a smile, "So you wanted to rescue the maiden from her master? What a brave, but foolish man."

"I did not know he was her master until later," Cooran replied sheepishly. "If I were not in prison, I would be willing to work to purchase this maiden's freedom."

The king pardons Norac's crime and tells him, "Norac, you must work for a season to repay the captain for the shame and humiliation you caused him."

Afterward, Norac is to resume his duties of maintaining the king's personal chariots. Cooran thanks the king and then excitedly heads for the captain's home. He looks forward to seeing the maiden again.

The captain is not happy with the king's decision but listens to Norac as he apologizes. Norac then offers to work beyond his sentence in order to purchase the maiden's freedom.

"That's impossible!" the captain tells him harshly. Then Delfar, the mistress of the house, walks in and adds coldly, "Myra has already been sold and taken far from this land."

Both Paninear and Delfar agreed that there was no need for Norac to work as payment for his actions against the captain. "The damage has already been done," they say.

Cooran leaves the captain's house deeply saddened that his beautiful maiden has been sold. He knows he may never see her again. In his thoughts he whispers, *Jah, please protect her as You have protected me.*

He resumes his position as the king's chariot keeper. But it is different now, because he and the king talk most intimately. The king is also saddened to hear of Norac's lost maiden and tells him how he too lost a precious jewel in his first wife and queen.

Several years have now passed, and the evil Queen Velmon takes ill and dies. The king mourns, but not for very long. Out of respect for her recent death, King Rohaan does not celebrate his own birthday that year. However, almost three months later, it is time to celebrate his dead son Cooran's birthday. In celebration, he asks Jacq, Nan, and Norac to be his special guests.

Cooran is especially delighted. He has decided that because this is his thirtieth birthday and the danger no longer hang over his life, he is ready to reveal his true identity. Cooran cuts his hair like that of his countrymen, shaves his beard, and dresses for the occasion. He carries his royally stamped birth certificate, rolled to fit through his mother's ring, as a gift to the king—his father.

Jacq and Nan are surprised by Norac's new look. Nan winks at him, already knowing his secret. Jacq's mouth drops open wide when he realizes how much Norac looks like King Rohaan. Cooran finally tells Jacq who he really is, just before they leave for the king's palace.

As the three men walk through the crowded streets heading toward the palace, joining other citizens, heads turn, fingers point, and whispers grow louder. When the three men walk into the king's outer courts, there, heads also turn in second looks at Norac. The atmosphere is festive with dancers, music, fire acts, and colorful performers. Finally, upon their arrival at the large doors leading to the ceremonial chamber, Jacq presents the guard with their special invitations.

As they enter the grand and beautifully decorated chamber, the crowd parts to let them through. Whispers spread through the large palace chamber, and then a hush comes over the crowd. King Rohaan, while greeting his guests, is immediately distracted by the unexpected silence. He looks up from his last greeted guest and sees a clean-shaven Norac approaching his throne. The king quickly greets his other guests, anxiously looking at Norac.

The three men, with big smiles, finally stand before the king seated on his throne. They then bow before him. King Rohaan stands up, with tears filling his eyes. He walks down several steps and asks, "Cooran? My son—Cooran?"

Cooran kneels as he presents the king with his gift. He then rises and warmly embraces his father for the first time and says,

**"Yes, Father, it is me, Cooran!"**

# REUNITED

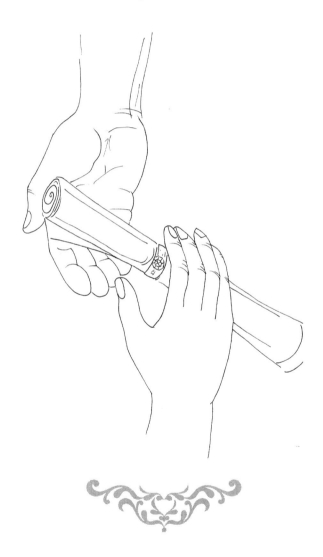

*I*n this beautiful land known as the kingdom of Daaveran, King Rohaan has just reunited with young Prince Cooran. Once it is noised abroad that the strong and gentle blacksmith Norac is actually the king's supposedly dead son, Cooran, the kingdom's celebration becomes even more jubilant. Most of his countrymen thought kindly toward him.

The celebrations continue for hours, lasting long into the early morning. There is dancing, singing, and fireworks, not only at the king's palace but at many of the homes in the kingdom. The king welcomes Cooran home to the palace. With tear-filled eyes, he joyously announces, "My son, who was once dead is now alive, and all is well."

Cooran thanks Jacq and his son, Nan, for their kindness to him over the years. The king offers places in the palace to both Jacq and Nan, but they decline. Even so, King Rohaan gives them privileged positions with free access to himself and his palace, along with a large reward. Nan and Cooran remain best friends.

During the following two years, Cooran and his father spend much time together. King Rohaan tells his son of his beautiful first wife, Cooran's mother, Queen Madeline, and how she died shortly after giving birth to him. "Cooran, I know she would have been a wonderful mother. She so looked forward to holding you in her arms and comforting you."

Cooran is warmed by the stories of his mother. He tells the king of his adoptive parents, Salamo and Merta, and the great love and kindness they poured on him. "They did not have much," Cooran says, "but they gave me their best, and for that I'm thankful."

"So am I," says the king.

Through the years, King Rohaan trains Cooran for his future reign over the kingdom. For most of his training, Cooran includes Nan, as his right-hand man. They learn numerous fighting techniques, military strategies, political procedures, and royal protocols. They even learn some other common, but simple languages. Many of the people in the kingdom love them both. But of course, Cooran's presence has now shifted the future order of some military powers.

As time goes on, the king sends Cooran and Nan on various ventures to other regions in his territory. Cooran discovers that his father's territory covers all the lands to the north and much of the lands to the west and south of Daaveran. During these travels, Cooran and Nan are amazed how far out of Daaveran their river runs. They venture very far to the south, far enough to see the river split into two separate rivers. However, going to the north, not as far away, their river divides into eight branches, of which seven branches extend to the great sea. Because of these river branches, citizens are drawn to the life these water veins provide and sustain. There are many small villages to their north, leading toward the great sea.

A great portion of the lands and territories going west and southward are ruled and governed by King Rohaan. Some of these are territories of dry and dusty inhabitants, while territories closer to the riverbanks have more lush vegetation and livestock. To the east is a smaller sea that stretches north and south, separating their kingdom from others.

During these ventures, Cooran has the experience of seeing other strange, new creatures he has only heard existed, including the river crocodiles, hippopotamus, long rodent-like creatures, others scaly and slithery, amphibians, and various birds. There are beautiful red lotus flowers that bloom during the months before the arrival of the colder season. And of course, there are the delicious date palms, acacia, sycamore, and tamarisk trees.

As part of his visits, Cooran presents strategies or relay

information to other leaders in these regions. In his many travels, Cooran secretly hopes to find the maiden that his heart longs for. He knows it is unlikely that he will find her. Even so, he holds on to that small speck of hope he feels deep within.

During one of his travel ventures, Cooran searches for a gift for his father, for upon his return, Daaveran will be celebrating the king's birthday. Cooran wants something special for his father. This is just before the start of the third year since Cooran and King Rohaan were reunited. In one of the territories, Cooran finds a chiseler of fine stones on a small and delicate scale. Cooran asks the chiseler to carve from a precious stone a form of the king with the queen holding their newborn baby. The piece is accented with pure gold and other precious stones. Cooran compliments the chiseler by telling him that the art piece is exquisite.

"This is perfect!" Cooran then exclaims, and Nan agrees.

When Cooran and Nan return, the king inquires of their success.

"It went well, Father," Cooran tells him.

The king then tells Cooran, "I have a task for you. I want you to review the cases of two of my servants I had thrown in prison some seasons ago and determine their fate." King Rohaan continues, "And we will give final judgment as part of my birthday celebration."

Cooran knows this is a heavy responsibility for him. He also knows that this will require great wisdom, since his judgment will mean life or death to these servants. The incidents for both cases took place within the same time period, where there appeared to be evil intent toward the royal family. This clearly angered the king, but because the evidence at the time was both insufficient and nebulous, King Rohaan imprisoned his servants rather than executing them immediately.

As Cooran thinks about this great task before him, he reflects back on a young friend he met many years ago. He called her "Little One." She had told him of her God, Jah, and how she trusted Him with her life and everything she did.

"Not only is Jah a good and merciful God, but Jah is also just," she had told him. "Trust Him! He will never lead you wrong."

Cooran decides to once again take his "little one's" advice. So he asks, "Jah, please guide me once again, for this is my greatest task yet. I trust You to guide me to make the right judgments."

Very early on the morning of the king's birthday, Cooran walks excitedly to his father's chamber with his gift. He wants to share time alone with his father before his much younger brothers and sisters or anyone else comes. His father is delighted to see Cooran and immediately knows what his gift represents.

Cooran tells the heart meaning of the special art piece he had made for his father. "Though we three have never been together at one time like this, there is and always will be a solid bond between us three."

King Rohaan says, "Thank you, son!" with a glimmer in his eyes and a tug at his heart.

They embrace as Cooran tells him, "I love you, Father."

As the day continues and the ceremonies are soon to begin, Cooran once again asks Jah for guidance, for wisdom, and for strength. His review of the cases and his judgments have already been determined, but he wants to be sure they are just and true.

The time comes for Cooran to give his judgments. The grand ceremonial chamber is filled with the citizens of Daaveran. On a platform to the left of King Rohaan's throne, stand the two former servants of the king, the chief cupbearer and the chief baker. Now, as prisoners, they await their final judgement. To the right of the king's throne, Cooran stands on a similar platform.

Then Prince Cooran proclaims:

> "To the chief of the cupbearers: In your attempt to please the king, you meant well by your deeds, but they were misunderstood, causing the king's wrath to come upon you. It is found that you meant no harm to the king or his courtiers. So return to your position as chief cupbearer."

Prince Cooran, then points to the next servant and says:

> "To the chief of the bakers: Your attempt was to look good before the king, but your heart was evil toward him. Your desire was for your position in the king's palace, but you had no regard for the safety and care of the king or his courtiers. Because your neglect and evil plot endangered the lives of the royal family and the courtiers, you will be executed this day, by hanging from a tree."

Through Cooran's prayers for guidance, a little research, and then some deep investigation into these matters, something quite interesting has come to light. Cooran uncovered a plot where Queen Velmon had colluded with the chief baker, a plot to harm the royal family. He also found that the chief cupbearer had not been involved but had been wrongly accused of neglect in her duties. This false allegation took place within the same time period, simply to divert any attention away from the chief baker. Even so, the wrath of the king's displeasure carried over to the chief baker as well, unaware of the queen's evil plot.

After Cooran's judgments are made, each is carried out and the festivities of the birthday celebration begins. King Rohaan beams with pride and agreement with Cooran's decisions and the quality of justice and wisdom with which he presented them.

Cooran grows stronger in his military and governing authority. King Rohaan has no concern about Cooran's ability to lead his kingdom when the time comes. However, the king has one concern. He tells Cooran, "Son, it is time you take a wife." He goes on, "It is time for you to start a family of your own, that our line will be strong."

"You are right, Father," Cooran replies. "And I have searched in every village, town, and kingdom I've visited, and I have yet to find the one I'm looking for."

"Do you still have hopes for that lost maiden?" the king asks softly, with a twinkle in his eyes. Cooran smiles but gives no reply.

"With your thirty-third birthday quickly approaching, we will have a grand ball and invite all the maidens for your choosing," the king said with excitement.

Cooran replies with a grin, "My king also needs a queen. If you find your queen, I promise to choose a maiden."

The king thinks it over and then responds with a hearty "Agreed!"

They both laugh.

The decree is sent to all unwed maidens, inviting them to Cooran's "Birthday Ball." In the meantime, Cooran has some traveling ventures to attend to with Nan. Though Cooran is not very excited, Nan, and many other young soldiers and men of the kingdom are delighted for their own marital opportunity. Currently, there is a shortage of maidens in the kingdom, and this Birthday Ball will be good for all. For that, Cooran is happy.

When the time for the Birthday Ball arrives, it is extravagant, elegant, and outrageously colorful and exciting. Maidens of all descriptions, origins, and attitudes are there. Many hearts are knitted together that night, even Nan's. But for the king and Cooran, no match is made.

As the festivities of Cooran's thirty-third birthday are coming to an end, King Rohaan shouts out giddily to Cooran, after his final dance, "I call a truce for now. But was this not fun?"

"This Birthday Ball? Indeed it was!" Cooran shouts back, out of breath. Then he bows before his last dance partner of the many lovely maidens he had previously danced.

The ball is festive and enjoyable, but Cooran is glad when it is finally over with. Nan and many of Daaveran's men are very happy, for this Ball has provided them with prospective mates.

Just days later, it is back to business as usual. Except many of the men are traveling back and forth to their maidens' homelands. Others are simply returning with their new wives by their sides. There is excitement in the air and all around. New life! New beginnings!

Now a full year and several seasons have passed. It is only a few days until time to celebrate the king's birthday once again. Cooran is preparing to take off on a short travel venture. That morning before he leaves, his father greets him with a disturbed look on his face.

Cooran asks jokingly, "Lonely or just a bad dream?"

"Something worse," the king responds with a smirk. "I had two bad dreams."

The king goes on to tell Cooran his dreams with a terribly puzzled look on his face. "I don't know what they mean, but they both seem to be some sort of sign." The king says, now frustrated.

"Father, I can't interpret your dreams, but I will pray to Jah for an answer for you."

The king scoffs, "I know not this god of yours you call Jah."

"Well, if it continues to bother you, Father, maybe you should consult your wise men and magicians," Cooran tells him. Then he is off with Nan.

While they are gone, the king continues to be troubled by his dreams. He ponders and says to himself, *My birthday celebration will not be enjoyable if I am unable to know the meaning of these dreams.*

Finally, he takes Cooran's advice and consults his magicians and his wise men. But no one is able to tell him what his dreams mean. King Rohaan becomes so distraught, he abruptly cancels his usually grand birthday celebration and threatens execution of his wise men and magicians. The king is restless all that day and the next. Throughout the nights, he is miserable and very troubled.

The chief cupbearer also has a terrible time sleeping that second night. Then she remembers how she has totally forgotten about someone special—the prisoner who interpreted her dream, as well as that of the chief of bakers, whiles sentenced to prison by the king. The chief cupbearer is now anxious to tell the king and impatiently waits for first light.

When dawn finally breaks the morning skies, the chief cupbearer quickly goes to the king. She tells him of an interpreter of dreams, who was once slave to the captain of the guard. Immediately, King Rohaan calls for this prisoner to come before him. Because of the urgency, the prisoner is hastily brought before the king. Though presentable, the prisoner is not properly groomed. Yet the king is struck with awe at her beauty. Even so, the king needs to first ease his troubled mind of these mysterious dreams of his.

So the king, though exhausted, anxiously tells the prisoner the details of his dreams.

> "In the first dream, I stood at the river as seven healthy, fat cows came out of the river. They soon began to feed in the meadow. Then, seven sickly, skinny cows came from out of the river near the healthy, fat cows. These sickly, skinny cows then ate up the healthy, fat cows, remaining as sickly and skinny as before. Then I awoke."

As King Rohaan continues, terror of his dreams shows on his face.

> "Then I slept and dreamed again. This time there were seven plump and good ears of corn that came up out of the stalk. Then sprung up seven thin and empty ears of corn that were blasted by the east wind. These thin and empty ears completely devoured the seven plump and good ears. They too remained thin and empty. After this, I awakened even more troubled by these dreams."

King Rohaan ends telling his dreams a bit shaken. He conveys his frustration that no one has been able to interpret these dreams, not even his magicians or his wise men. Then he says, with a sigh of hope, "I was told that you are able to understand dreams and to interpret them."

The prisoner, who is called Sephina, lets the king know that she is unable to interpret his dreams on her own, but her God, Jah, will give the king an answer to ease his troubled mind. Now the king is even more eager to hear the interpretation of his dreams. He has heard references to this foreign god, called Jah, not long ago from his son. "Who is this 'Jah'?" the king roughly asks. "I do not know nor do I serve this god of yours."

Sephina quickly yet firmly tells the king about her God and then begins to give the meaning of his dreams. "The two dreams are really one, but because it will soon come to pass, Jah wants to make this known to the king."

She continues, "The seven healthy, fat cows and the plump, good ears of corn are seven years of abundance and great harvest. The seven sickly, skinny cows and the thin, empty ears of corn are seven years of destructive famine."

King Rohaan's demeanor softens as he hears his dreams unfold. A profound peace begins to come over him.

Then Sephina tells him, "King Rohaan, the latter seven years are the plans of the evil one to destroy your kingdom. The former seven years will be Jah's provision as preparation for this time of devastation. Jah has also given a plan to successfully counteract the evil one's intent of death and devastation and to save your kingdom." She then explains the plan to the king as Jah reveals it to her.

King Rohaan warmly thanks Sephina and orders that she be well taken care of, with a resting chamber in the palace. Later, Sephina is to dine with the king, his son, and his courtiers and officials. Until then, she remains free to roam within the confines of the palace courtyards. After she leaves, King Rohaan gives orders that a small birthday feast be prepared.

Then he ponders the interpretation of the dreams and the plan given by the prisoner. He earlier inquires from his wise men and magician of any such phenomena of past lengthy famines or times of great crops. They cannot find any similar occurrence. Strangely enough, the king senses a new peace deep within. His torment is gone, and he concludes that he will accept this maiden's words as both reliably sound interpretation and as valuable information.

Besides, this interpretation is much more than the king received from his own wise men or magicians. He acknowledges to himself that he can even see with some clarity how the interpretation connects with both his dreams. And the plan revealed has merit. Though these seven-year events seem rather unlikely, the king believes it would prove wise to prepare for the predicted worst.

However, King Rohaan surmises that the validity of this interpretation will be proven soon enough by the yield of this year's or next year's crops. As was told, these events are soon to take place. So it would be wiser to follow the plan and prepare for such a yield, rather than wait for proof and expose his kingdom to the potential threat of a devastating famine. If there are no abundant crops, then the interpretation will be deemed false, and the plan will come to a halt.

And Cooran! King Rohaan begins to consider how these great events might be attributed to the same strange god his son Cooran has been telling him about. Since their reunion a few years earlier, Cooran has often credited Jah for the wisdom in his decision-making and judgments in the courts. Though profoundly pleased with Cooran's abilities in the courts, the king admits how foolish he thinks it is for anyone to believe that there could be only "one true god." King Rohaan never discouraged Cooran in his beliefs, but he can never see himself believing such foolishness. Still, he remembers that Cooran told him that Jah can be trusted and that He loves and has concern for all His creation—which is exactly what this maiden said about her God, Jah.

In addition, his chief cupbearer assured him of the accuracy of Sephina's interpretations of both her own dream and the chief baker's dream. King Rohaan feels it prudent now to take the leap of believing this interpretation as valid, rather than denying it and later finding his kingdom in danger.

Though this is a dreadful situation, the king is relieved to finally know what his dreams mean and also to have a plan to save his people. He is thrilled with all this new knowledge. Yet he foresees that if this plan of Jah's is to be successful, he needs a wise overseer able to lay out the plan and make it work. It does not take him long to determine whom he will appoint to oversee this great task. With Cooran soon to return, the king wants to wait, in order to confer with his son before presenting his thoughts to his top officials and announcing his appointment. Even though the plan was given by a god he does not know, the king is deeply grateful to have this god know him. He even agrees with the maiden when she says that Jah is both good and wise.

When Cooran returns several hours later, King Rohaan is anxious to meet with his young prince before meeting with the top officials of his kingdom. As Cooran approaches the throne and bows, the king asks, with an excited smile, "How was your journey?"

But before his son can answer, the king tells him with great delight, "I have the answers; I've got *all* the answers."

Cooran looks up with great surprise and asks, "Father, you have the answer to both of your dreams?"

The king says excitedly, "I've got the answer to my dreams and a whole lot more. Let's go to my chamber to discuss this before we meet with the others."

They both proceed to the king's chamber, where King Rohaan freely dances with delight. Cooran is surprised at the delightful change of his father's mood from the depressed man he left behind a few days before. As they greeted each other, Cooran wanted to embrace his father but restrained himself, since he was still dusty from his short, hard journey.

King Rohaan tells his son of the unbelievably great things that took place during his absence from Daaveran. He tells Cooran the meaning of his dreams, the plan that was given to save his people and his kingdom, and the person he has chosen to make sure this plan works. Finally he tells Cooran about the beautiful maiden, once a servant to the captain of the guard, who had told him of her God—Jah, who gave the dreams, the interpretation, the plan, and its overseer.

King Rohaan, now bursting with excitement, then announces, "And this maiden is perfect for you, Cooran! She will make you a fine wife."

Dumbfounded, Cooran responds, "And you have known her for how long? All of several hours, and you now know that she is perfect for me?" Cooran whines, "Father!"

"Let me meet with the other officials for a final discussion, and then we shall all dine with this maiden, Sephina, and you will see!"

"Sephina?" Cooran asks, totally confused.

"Yes, that is the maiden's name," King Rohaan says. "Did I not tell you?"

"Sephina! No, it can't be." Cooran thinks out loud. "It's ... it's not possible."

The king now looks rather puzzled himself, but is still smiling with excitement.

"Father, did you say her God is Jah?" Cooran asks slowly.

"Yes, Jah is His Name!" and in unison they say, "and He is a good and wise God." They look at each other in utter amazement.

King Rohaan then informs his son that he plans to make the special announcement during his birthday feast. Cooran is thankful, excited, yet confused by all the information his father has shared with him. In all the confusion, Cooran has almost forgotten his gift to his father. He presents him with a rather large bundle wrapped in a special cloth. Smiling broadly as he leaves the king's chambers, Cooran tells his father, "Special birthday greetings! Now with answers to your dreams, you can truly enjoy your celebration."

Again, Cooran wants to embrace his father there and then. But he wishes to first refresh himself from the dust of his travels, before his father's announcement and birthday feast. King Rohaan smiles with delight as Cooran leaves. The king unwraps his gift and gasps with excitement. Then he leaves to meet with his top officials.

Cooran quickly goes to refresh himself before heading to the dining chamber. As he cleans up and changes his attire, he is giddy with excitement at the possibility of his "little one" being here in the land of his birth. Cooran looks in the mirror, deep in thought. He had been confused because, as his father described the maiden, his first thought was of the maiden Myra, he had longed to find. But it could not be her, since she was sold to travelers from outside Daaveran. Now, it sounds like this maiden may actually be his friend from years long past. But how can that be? Sephina, a prisoner?

Cooran shakes his head quizzically and says out loud, "No way this maiden could be my Sephina." He hesitates and thinks, *Nah ... no way!* Then he hurries to the celebration.

As King Rohaan meets with his top officials, he discusses the situation. He tells them how his dreams reveal a period to come, having seven years of plenty, with good harvests, and then seven years of famine—no rain and no full harvest. Nothing but death and suffering can be expected, if Jah's plan is not properly followed.

One official questions the validity of the interpretation. However, another official reasons that the king's strange dreams would appear to be some kind of sign. He then proposes that precautions be taken, lest it could otherwise be proven that there is no possible threat to the kingdom. With that, everyone agrees to follow the plan.

The king tells them about the maiden Sephina and how impressed he is by her ability to interpret dreams, her confidence in her God, and her beauty. He lightly jokes about appointing her to Cooran as his wife. They all chuckle.

Receiving the interpretation of the king's dreams, as well as the instructions to save their kingdom, is a welcome relief to the king's top officials. But coming from a foreign god ... well, that is quite unusual. Still, everyone is truly grateful and intrigued about the interpreter of dreams. They all acknowledge that the task to follow the plan will be a great challenge, requiring real wisdom and much organization.

King Rohaan, immediately addressing the concerned looks evident on their faces, announces, "I must appoint someone to oversee this daunting project." Then he says with a gleam in his eyes and with great delight, "Actually, I have already decided who that will be."

The king then shares with them his chosen appointee. They all agree that the king has made the perfect choice. King Rohaan tells them that he will explain the situation and announce his choice for the task to the rest of his courtiers and leaders, during his birthday feast, now being prepared.

They all leave to quickly refresh themselves before joining

the others in the dining chamber. Everyone is happy that the king is no longer tormented by his strange dreams, excited about the unexpected celebration and announcement, and thrilled to meet their special guest, Sephina.

Convening just an hour later, King Rohaan and his top officials head to the dining chamber together. Cooran, on the other hand, arrives by himself. He got so caught up in his thoughts, he believes he is the last to arrive at the dining chamber. When Cooran finally joins the others, their special guest has not yet arrived. So Cooran then has ample time to embrace his father with a big "Happy birthday!" squeeze. King Rohaan is proudly wearing a dazzlingly ornate robe, which was in the large bundle Cooran recently gave him. Cooran beams with affection.

Just as they sit, the large and beautifully carved wooden double doors open, announcing their special guest. As she enters the dining chamber, all the men stand and are in awe of her beauty. This time Sephina has properly been pampered and groomed. She had been given a beautiful dinner gown—totally form fitting, as is the customary attire for the women of Daaveran—to dine with the royal courtiers and leaders of this kingdom. Sephina too is in awe of the grandeur of the palace and her surroundings, and to be there is truly remarkable.

Before interpreting the king's dreams only hours ago, Sephina had spent more than five long years in the king's prison. She had falsely been accused by her previous masters. And nearly a decade before that, she had been sold into slavery by her very own sisters. Now, here she stands before this kingdom's royalty in the king's palace. Sephina's thoughts immediately turn to the faithfulness and truth of Jah, the God whom she serves and trusts with her very life. Thinking excitedly to herself of how amazing Jah is, Sephina then whispers, "Jah, You are so faithful."

Sephina is not yet aware, but she is being escorted to be seated next to King Rohaan and his son, Prince Cooran. As she comes closer, Cooran smiles excitedly, thinking that his father might be right in saying that she is perfect for him. Then, to his surprise, he recognizes her as the beautiful maiden he has searched for in every village, town, territory, and kingdom he has traveled over the years.

A few years earlier, he had only seen this maiden from a distance, unable to meet and befriend her. But now here she is, walking toward him. He then asks himself if this is the maiden his father told him of. Though he is rather excited, he is again puzzled, because he had hoped from his father's description that she might be a friend from his youth. He is now totally confused; yet the mysterious maiden is being escorted ever closer to him.

Then Sephina stops in mid-stride and says just above a whisper, "Cooran?" His mind races and is dizzy with confusion, as he sees her lips form his name.

Cooran moves from the table toward her, as everyone looks on in utter surprise. He now knows her, but not as the mysterious and beautiful maiden he first recognized. *It is ... is it really?* ... He then softly calls out, "Sephina? My 'little one'—is that really you?"

Everyone is surprised! The king is so excited he can hardly contain himself. Smiling! Laughing! Cooran and Sephina run toward each other. They both stop short, looking incredulously at each other. And then they embrace.

*Old friends ~ Reunited!*

# APPOINTED BY THE KING

*E*veryone cheers and laughs with them as Cooran escorts Sephina to her chair. Once she sits, all the men sit too. Then King Rohaan asks with great surprise, "Cooran, do you know the maiden Sephina?" They both look at each other and smile uncontrollably.

Cooran finally says excitedly, "This is Sephina, my 'little one' from my youth, whom I told you about." Then he says more adoringly, "But she's not so little anymore."

With that, King Rohaan abruptly and joyfully stands up and introduces Sephina to all his courtiers and leaders. Everyone claps and cheers again. Then the king pronounces, "Well then, let the feast begin." And dinner is served with all sorts of meats, delicacies, and lots of this kingdom's produce.

Cooran and Sephina have a great deal of catching up to do. It is utterly amazing and truly unbelievable—the two of them in the king's palace, the place of Cooran's birth.

As the dessert is to be served, King Rohaan stands, telling everyone what he dreamt and the interpretation to his troubling dreams. The chamber becomes noisy with concerns. To know of extraordinarily abundant crops for a full seven years is wonderful; and to then understand that their kingdom can be utterly destroyed over the following seven years by famine: what a dilemma!

Then the king says, "Attention, everyone! We have been given a great plan to deliver us." He smiles. "Now the time has come to appoint someone for this great task at hand."

He continues, "From my dreams and the information Sephina's God, Jah, provided through her, know that the task to save our kingdom will be great. Know also that such a great task will require someone with much wisdom to see it to a successful end."

King Rohaan then breathes deep and says with great pride, "I now appoint"—he pauses—"Sephina to oversee our newest and greatest challenge." Everyone stands, claps, and cheers.

Sephina sits smiling, quite surprised, yet honored and a bit overwhelmed. As they grow quiet, the king continues. "My top officials and I have agreed that Sephina is the best person for this task. We believe that if her God, Jah, used her to interpret my dreams, entrusted her to deliver the danger warning, and provided her the instructions to save our kingdom, He will then properly enable her to successfully manage the task to its completion."

Then King Rohaan adds, "And for the mercies, goodness, and wisdom of Jah toward me and our kingdom, I give Him great thanks!" At that, Sephina stands, and everyone lifts their chalices and says, "Thanks be to Jah, the God of Sephina!"

As the king continues, everyone sits, now feeling an assured hope. King Rohaan turns and gives Sephina a signet ring, signifying her appointed position to be second only to himself. This position is to be above all his top officials, even above Prince Cooran. The responsibility of the task before her is so great and so important to the survival of the kingdom that no one objects, at least not openly. Nor does anyone seem offended by the king's appointment of Sephina to this position. King Rohaan provides Sephina a chamber in the palace in which to stay until a home of her own is prepared. All her needs will be met. Whatever Sephina needs or desires will be hers.

Once the appointment is complete, the king stands with a great smile as his birthday cake is brought in and the singing begins. Adding many other desserts, loud cheering, and much clashing of chalices, the birthday celebration is now in full swing. Seeing Prince Cooran and Sephina together delights the king. With a final thought, King Rohaan reflects how great his birthday celebration has turned out to be after all.

While the celebration continues inside the palace, Prince Cooran leads Sephina to the outdoor courtyards. There they walk and talk for hours, even until the early morning.

Cooran first congratulates Sephina on her appointment. "You have been appointed to the second highest position today. I am so very happy for you." He takes her hands and gives them a gentle squeeze. "The task ahead will be a difficult one, but I know Jah will make you most successful."

He smiles almost uncontrollably and continues. "Oh, it is so wonderful to see you again, Sephina." As he spins her around, he tells her, "And you truly are not so little anymore. Look how you've grown," he says with a wide, soft smile.

Sephina replies, "I had no idea that you were the Cooran whose birthday was celebrated throughout the kingdom all these years— though hearing the name always brought special memories of you." She continues, gently scolding him, "You never told me you were a prince."

He tells her his story, starting from his birth, leading to his journey after he had left her and her family many years before. He tells her how Jah protected him through numerous occasions, just as she had told him He would. Then he goes on to tell her what took place upon his return to this, his birthplace. He shares how he used his adoptive name, Norac, and worked for many years as a blacksmith, hiding his identity until he thought it safe.

"What? Norac, the blacksmith?" Sephina asks, bewildered, as she closely studies Cooran's face. She touches his smooth cheeks gently. "You are Norac? I'd so hoped to one day see Norac again, to thank him for rescuing me from my master." Sephina then says, "And it was you, Cooran. I did not know." Her voice is soft and tender. "Thank you! Thank you so very much."

She goes on to tell him how she ended up in his kingdom. "My loving sisters decided to sell me, rather than kill me," she says with a chuckle. "You warned me to deal wisely with them, but I guess I was not wise enough."

"But you trusted Jah," Cooran comments with joy. "And look at you now! Jah brought you right here, right now! Wow! How awesome is that?"

They walk a little farther and then settle on a bench. Sephina begins to tell the story of her life in Daaveran.

"When I arrived here, I was sold to one of your officials—the captain of the guard and his wife, as you now know. I worked in my masters' fields for a little more than four years and then over three and a half years in and around their home. Because of Jah's favor toward me, the mistress gave me full authority over everything in the house and the fields.

"In the latter part of my second year in that position, the master of the house began to show more interest in me than he should. Sometime afterwards, he threatened that he had plans to take me to another province, where I would become his second wife. I prayed to Jah for help, that it would never be so."

Sephina continues, "The day that Norac—you—rescued me, once the master returned home, he and my mistress argued with each other throughout that very night. The next day, my mistress accused me of stealing and had me taken to prison."

She sighs and says with a smile, "But I knew that Jah was with me, and I continued to trust Him. I've been in the king's prison ever since, until this very day," she says with a big smile. "Jah took what the evil one planned would destroy me and turned it around for my good. In being sent to prison, I could not be forced to be my master's mistress."

"Jah truly is the one true God," Cooran says, gently squeezing her hand.

"Oh yes, He is!" Sephina agrees with delight, realizing that he has entrusted his own life to Jah.

Cooran tells her how he came to trust Jah through the years—especially while he, too, was in prison, after his attempt to rescue her, the mysterious maiden. "Jah had proven Himself to be true," he says.

There was an old prisoner who recognized him by the small scar that was on Cooran's upper right cheek. This scar was visible just above the thick facial hair he wore during those years he hid his identity.

"This prisoner was once the servant to the queen. She had ordered him to kill me when I was only a lad and to burn my body." He goes on to tell how the queen had struck him, Cooran, on the face. Her ring left a small scar on his cheek. It was first his eyes and then this scar that the old servant identified the prince.

The old servant ended up in prison years later, once the queen discovered that he had not killed Cooran. The ashes the servant had given the queen as evidence of the child's death were those of an animal. The queen tried to force the old servant to tell her of Cooran's whereabouts.

"When he did not or could not, the queen had his tongue removed and ordered him thrown into prison. There the old servant stayed, until I revealed my identity and asked the king's pardon for the servant." The king gladly released the old servant, seeing that he had rescued his son from death. Cooran continues telling Sephina how the old servant was given a place in the king's palace but died only a year later.

"It was during my time in prison, when I realized that Jah had protected me even then. The old servant first pointed at and then touched my scar. He was thrilled to see that I had lived to become a man, yet heartbroken to see me in prison. He began to write in the dirt when we were alone, telling me his story."

Cooran shares with her how the old servant began to tell of Jah, the God of his father's father. The grandfather of the old servant had encountered Jah during a stranger's visit to their kingdom (a neighboring kingdom just outside one of Daaveran's territories) many, many years before. The story was passed on to the old servant from his father's father, down to him.

Cooran continues, "He said that this stranger's God, Jah, was powerful, forgiving, and good. The servant told how Jah had closed the wombs of their women when the king his grandfather served took the stranger's wife for himself. Jah forgave the king once he restored this woman back to her husband. Then Jah opened the wombs of all their women once again.

"The old servant explained how his father's mother, who had been barren earlier, was then able to conceive and bore a precious son, the old servant's father. Because of such a gift, his father's father and mother both believed in and trusted Jah as their own God. His father shared this story with him, and he too trusted and believed in Jah. For this reason, the old servant could not bear to take the life of an innocent little lad, no matter who gave the orders.

"Sephina, I had also prayed to Jah to protect the beautiful maiden I tried to rescue and hoped to one day see again. I had no idea that she was you. And now that I do, I'm even more thankful for Jah's protection over you."

As the days turn into months, it is not long before preparations begin for the kingdom's grand celebration of Prince Cooran's birthday. He and Sephina continue spending time together, whenever they have the opportunity. He is still traveling as before, and she has started her new role of overseeing The Great Harvest Plan, as they now call it. She too will eventually have to travel throughout the kingdom of Daaveran and its territories to determine the ideal locations for future storage and distribution centers.

Sephina follows the instructions of the plan that Jah gave her and trusts Him to guide her with all the necessary details as well. The plan itself is basic, yet extensive, giving new ideas for planting, harvesting, storing, and preserving grains, water, and other commodities. Jah gives her wisdom to determine what all will be needed. She is able to figure out how much land should be planted, which locations will be best suited for the crops, what type of seeds will be best to plant, the different tasks that will be required, how many workers and animals will be needed to perform these tasks, where to place these workers and animals, how to arrange adequate storage and protection of the harvested goods, when and how to distribute the goods, and the proper timing of it all. This is only the beginning.

Yes, the task before her is great. Now it is time to put the plan to work. Then Sephina says with great joy, "Thank You, Jah, for Your great plan. Special thanks for Your guidance to bring all these things together." Sephina thinks of how she has continually put her trust in Jah and then says to herself, with a big smile, *And He has never failed me, not even once, throughout all these years.*

During Cooran's most recent trip, he confides in Nan, his second-in-command and confidant. He tells Nan how his heart has been totally captivated by Sephina. Though he knows that Sephina cares deeply for him, he is not sure that her heart aches the same for him.

Nan chides him, "You are the prince. You can have your father give her to you—maybe as a birthday gift." Nan chuckles as he continues. "He did once say that she is perfect for you, right?"

"Yes, this is all true," Cooran soberly replies. "But I want this to be her desire as well."

Nan then suggests, "Why don't you simply express your heart to her? That way you can determine how she feels toward you." Cooran considers this as a sensible approach.

When Cooran returns from his travels, he immediately goes to see Sephina. She has been busy with her tasks, but she is delighted to see him. He asks her if they could meet after dinner that evening to discuss a pressing matter. She gladly agrees.

At the palace, Cooran goes to see his father, the king. They greet each other with their usual warm embrace. The king asks him, "Was your travel successful? You seem troubled about something."

"Father, all went well," Cooran tells the king. "But I do have a matter I want to discuss with you in private."

So they retreat to the king's chamber. "What is it, my son?" the king asks with concern in his voice.

"Father, my heart aches for Sephina," Cooran confesses to him. "I want to have her as my bride."

King Rohaan immediately jumps up with delight and says, "I told you she is perfect for you. So why are you troubled? I will announce the appointment tonight at dinner."

"No, Father! I first want to know Sephina's heart toward me. I don't want to be appointed her husband or she my wife. I want her to want me, as I want her." He continues, "I will speak with her tonight."

"As you wish, but I know her heart is for you as well, Cooran," the king says, beginning to dance with laughter and delight. Then he sings, "My son will soon marry."

At dinner, King Rohaan is all smiles, though Cooran is rather quiet. Sephina is delighted to have Cooran back at the palace, after his absence for almost two weeks. She has noticed her longings for his returns. When he visited her earlier as she worked, she wished to have given him a great big embrace to welcome him home. She waited anxiously for the time to pass, so she could see him at dinner. Now she sits next to him, but he has been quiet and rather serious all during dinner, not at all like himself.

Suddenly, Sephina becomes concerned, knowing that he wants to speak with her after dinner. *Is something wrong?* she wonders. Her heart aches suddenly, not knowing what he may have to tell her. She then calms her mind and speaks under her breath, "I trust You, Jah, even with my beloved Cooran."

Sephina has noticed that for the past month or so, her heart has grown beyond fondness towards her gentle young friend of years ago, Cooran. Her fondness developed for him after he rescued her from possibly becoming dinner to some wild beast. Her heart toward him has even grown beyond adoration for the strong Norac, who rescued her from her master's grip. She now wants to give her heart and her life totally to this most wise and wonderful man, her best friend, Cooran.

Finally, dinner is over. Cooran escorts Sephina once again to their favorite place to be together, the courtyards of the palace. The moon is full and bright and the night air cool but soft. They walk for a while in silence and then stop to look out over the kingdom of Daaveran, under the beautiful moonlit sky.

Then Sephina finally asks with concern in her voice, "Cooran, you have a pressing matter. What is it?"

He turns to face her and looks deeply into her beautiful almond-shaped eyes in silence. He takes her hands into his own and says, "Sephina, I once cherished you as my 'little one'—a little sister and friend I didn't have. I even took your advice to trust Jah with my life. I'm so thankful I did."

He continues, "I admired you from a distance, as my mysterious and beautiful maiden, though I didn't realize she was you. Now I've come to see you as my best friend, even closer than my father or Nan."

He firmly but gently squeezes her hands and then draws them to his chest. He tells her, "Sephina, my heart longs for you, and I desire you to become one with me. I know you care deeply for me as a friend, but I'm not sure if your heart aches for me as my heart aches for you."

Sephina is so touched by his words that she stands speechless. Tears begin to fill her eyes, and she finally speaks. "Cooran, as Jah gives me breath, my heart, my mind, my very being wishes to be completely yours."

With this, Cooran softly kisses her hands. With a sigh of pure delight, he gently wipes the tears from her face. He then asks, "Sephina, will you have me as your husband and lover and honor me in becoming my bride and sole companion?"

Sephina begins to weep. As tears stream down her cheeks, she answers him softly, but firmly, "Oh yes, Cooran! Yes, I will!" They embrace, and he gently lifts her from the ground and spins around.

The following morning, the king sends out a decree—a grand announcement, stating:

*"This day, I, King Rohaan, of Daaveran,*
*Do Hereby Proudly APPOINT:*
*My Son, PRINCE COORAN,*
*as Husband to SEPHINA*
*and My Second-in-Command, SEPHINA,*
*as Wife to PRINCE COORAN."*

# THE INVITATIONS

I ~ King Rohaan
of the Kingdom of Daaveran
do hereby Invite You to the
Grand Celebration of
The Royal Union of

Prince TOORAN

My Son

&

SEPHINA

My Second-in-Command

*P*roudly and with great joy, King Rohaan has recently sent out the following decree announcing a special union.

> *This day,*
> *I, King Rohaan, of Daaveran,*
> *Do Hereby Invite You to Celebrate*
> *The UNION of*
> *PRINCE COORAN, my son,*
> *&*
> *SEPHINA, My Second-in-Command!"*

Immediately thereafter, instead of the usual grand birthday celebration for Prince Cooran, an extravagant wedding is quickly planned. Invitations are sent to all the territories under the king's rule and neighboring kingdoms. Much planning and preparation are completed in just a little less than a month's time.

During this time of wedding preparations, Sephina continues her work on the task that will someday save the kingdom from the destructive famine, predicted to last for seven long years. Before this famine, there are to be seven years of abundant harvests. It is the proper management and coordination of these great harvests that will see them through the period of the destructive famine. Both of these events were foretold to the king through his dreams. Sephina has already laid out the plans, yet much work still lies ahead to prepare for both the good years of harvests and the destructive years of famine.

Cooran, on the other hand, has been busy traveling to the territories under his father's rule. He has the responsibility of overseeing the wise governing of these territories. He also has to make and keep good relations with neighboring kingdoms. He is especially called upon to make the major and final judgments over criminal and civil issues in all the lands under his father's rule. His work has become more and more demanding. He is always looking for good leaders in each territory who may assist him with his responsibilities.

Both Cooran and Sephina have been very busy, each with their own tasks. So they welcome the interruptions to help in preparations for the ceremony of their union. Occasionally they sneak away for some quiet time alone. Usually they spend this time at their favorite meeting place, the courtyards of the king's palace. Most special is a particular section of the courtyard which overlooks the kingdom.

Cooran and Sephina stroll through the gardens holding hands, occasionally talking, often just walking in silence. At times, they just sit and look out at the moonlit skies, gazing at the soft lights of the kingdom below. More often they get lost staring deeply into each other's eyes, with excitement and joy. Their love for each other grows deeper with each passing moment. They both continuously thank Jah for bringing them together.

Finally, the time has arrived for their union. Tomorrow, they will wed. People from near and far will be there to celebrate with them. Sephina, though the happiest she has ever been, has a hidden sadness still. She longs for her father and her family to share in her most joyous occasion. But it is not to be so.

Sephina, many years ago, was sold into slavery by her very own sisters. Though she endured horrible times as a slave, she gives thanks—especially during hard times—to Jah, her God, whom she trusts fully. She believes that Jah is with her at all times. She also believes that Jah uses even the deeds of the evil one for His own purposes and the good of His people. For Jah's purposes, Sephina has grown from her father's favorite little girl and the most hated by her sisters, to a young attractive slave and prisoner. From her position as slave and prisoner, Jah has now brought her to the position of Second-in-Command, subject only to the king of this great realm. And very soon, to add delight to a prominent position, Jah has granted Sephina—a most beautiful and mature maiden—the honor to wed the most handsome and wise prince of this kingdom. How faithful is her God, Jah? Oh! Ever so faithful!

The night before they are to wed, shortly after dinner, Cooran takes Sephina's hands as he leads her for a stroll through the courtyard's garden. They both breathe deeply as they walk out into the fresh night air. The skies are dotted with twinkling stars, and the fragrance of flowers fills the air.

Cooran stops. Looking into her eyes, he says, "Sephina, tomorrow we shall become one." He continues with a big smile, "I so look forward to spending the rest of my days with you by my side and in my arms." Sephina is silent, for her eyes are filled with tears of joy, and she fears she'll sob if she says anything. Cooran gently wipes the tears from her face, and they embrace.

The next morning, Sephina awakens to the aroma of a wonderful, hot breakfast being brought to her chamber. Even so, she is too excited to eat much of anything. Also brought into her chamber, and hung near a window that is now flooded with brilliant sunrays, is the most dazzling wedding gown she has ever seen.

It is a pearly white gown that cascades from the shoulders to the floor. The gown has no sleeves, but has a separate collar that is made of the same pearly white satin cloth, embroidered with an intertwining gold and silver design, accented with rare pearls. This collar sits from the inner shoulder, just barely covering the outer shoulders, across the upper back and chest. The edging of this collar has a solid gold-colored embroidery, with embellished gold-like ball droplets, dangling along all the edges. A similarly designed belt is just as broad, but without the dangling gold droplets. This belt goes around the waist, then hangs in the front below the waist to just above the knees. Though the gown is form fitting, it flares behind the knees, leaving a trail of pearly white cloth that flows several feet onto the floor.

Accompanying the gown is a simple yet elegantly designed crown. She is told that this crown once belonged to Queen Madeline, Cooran's mother. There are long twirling transparent ribbons of sapphire, emerald, topaz, and ruby, attached to the rear of the crown, to add color and vibrancy as they flow down the back of an already exquisite gown. These ribbons will also accentuate the jewels that will be placed in her hair. With a gasp, she says, "Oh my, how beautiful!"

The reality that this gown was made especially for her, and that she is soon to become Princess Sephina, is all quite overwhelming. Even this realization seems small in the awesomeness of Jah's great love and faithfulness towards her.

A few short hours later, the air is filled with the sounds of many horns blaring and the deep beat of drums. They announce the gathering of the kingdom's residents and visitors from miles around, assembling for the grand celebration. The atmosphere is magnificent, with a great number of people from various tribes, creeds, and cultures. There are thousands dressed in their very best and the courtiers in their colorful royal apparel. The air is fresh, crisp, and clean, filled with excitement and great joy. It is cheerfully noisy with chatter and music.

In the open outer courtyards where the guests arrive, the scenery is delightful. Peacocks walk proudly as they display their vibrant feathers. There are very big, beautiful, tamed, and well-fed cats with stripes, spots, or just plain shiny coats. Several of these cats are native to the kingdom and surrounding territories, while others are gifts from distant kingdoms. Some of these cats lie in the shade purring as others regally stroll through the crowds panting. They each lead around a caretaker, and these hold strong cords attached to each cat's jeweled collar.

There are rare and colorful birds singing, chirping, or just plain squawking. Some are flying, while most are perched on the beautifully decorated fences. These fences stand tall on either side of the outer courtyard and are covered in an assortment of white flowers, dotted with tiny red and pink rosebuds.

Many servants offer refreshing drinks, sweet cakes, and fruits to the throng. Other servants wave long staffs tipped with ostrich feathers, fanning and cooling the guests. Soon the ceremony will begin.

The time has come, and the guests now parade into the grand ceremonial chamber of the palace. This chamber is decorated with rainbows of wide, translucent ribbons draped high above the crowd. Each window is outlined with white jasmine and water lilies, sprinkled with lotus buds of white, red, and pink, and accented with the fully bloomed red lotus flowers. There are soft and very thin sheets covering the windows, allowing the cool breezes and the soft sunrays to freely flow into the ceremonial chamber.

Cooran proudly stands before their guests, on a platform just in front of the throne of King Rohaan. His heart races as he anxiously awaits the opening of the chamber doors concealing his bride from view. Now he breathes deeply, wanting to take in every second when Sephina emerges into the ceremonial chambers.

Cooran wears the traditional shendyt—a short wrap that falls from just below his waist to inches above his knees. The shendyt is made of a heavy off-white linen cloth, with strands of gold woven throughout. The tail of the shendyt is trimmed with a thick embroidered gold band, which trails upward as it wraps from the front center to the side of the shendyt. The wide bronze-colored waistband is like an ornate belt with dazzling jewels of emeralds, sapphire, and rubies all around. And from the center front hangs a similar beltlike band that widens slightly as it descends, falling just below the shendyt's length. But instead of jewels, this band has intricate design patterns woven throughout, with a buckle-like scarab at the top and a smaller scarab at the shendyt's tail.

Falling from around Cooran's neck to just above his shoulders is a handsomely beaded collar, stringed with gold, accented with bronze and dazzling jewels like those of his belts. His muscular arms and wrists have coordinating bands. His sandals, made of braided papyrus and palm leaves, are specially designed with smaller but coordinating bands. His golden-bronze robe, made from transparently thin linen, softly drapes across his shoulders, accentuating his golden-brown complexion and hazel colored eyes. After the ceremony, this robe will be worn more cape-like, as it will drape from the center back of his beaded collar to the floor.

And finally, Cooran's headdress. It too is made from the heavy off-white linen cloth with the interwoven gold strands. However, it has alternating stripes colored golden-bronze. This headdress drapes the whole head, with each sidepiece falling like large braids on Cooran's chest. At the base and around the forehead of this headdress sits his gold crown, embedded with several precious stones.

At last, the trumpets sound, and everyone falls silent. Next, all stand and hold their breath for the final trumpet to announce the bride's entrance. Then, slowly, as the single trumpet is blown, the special doors within the ceremonial chamber are opened. Out fly three white doves, and there Sephina stands. She is truly beautiful and glows most radiantly.

She slowly glides down a path, covered with red poppy and rose petals, between the guests. The jewels braided into her hair cast dazzling lights across the chamber's walls, and her dress glistens as the sunrays envelop her. As Sephina walks toward her groom, it seems the sunlight illumines each step she takes.

The crowd stands in awe, as soft music plays in the background. Then Cooran walks down the aisle to meet his approaching bride. With arms extended forward and a joyous smile, he loudly proclaims as he walks, "I, Cooran, invite you, Sephina, to join with me." He turns as he reaches her side, takes her right arm onto his left, and escorts her to the platform before the king. As they walk arm in arm, occasionally glancing at each other, Sephina speaks softly for Cooran's hearing, "Happy birthday, my love!" His smile broadens as he looks upon his beautiful bride.

Then they stand before King Rohaan and proclaim their love for and to each other, each vowing their commitment to the other for as long as they both live. They turn face to face, each holding the other's hands.

As they look into each other's eyes, Cooran begins, "I, Cooran, invite you, Sephina, not only to walk by my side, but to share my life. I invite you into my heart and into all that I am." And he continues as he squeezes her hands, "Sephina, I invite you to be my wife and my life companion. I invite you to be the mother of my children and to be my best friend for life."

Now, with tears filling her eyes, Sephina boldly proclaims, "I, Sephina, wholeheartedly and gladly accept this great invitation of yours, Cooran. I vow to love and to respect you in all that I say and do. I, Sephina, long to become one with you, Cooran, as my husband and my best friend."

King Rohaan finalizes their union by asking them, "In sealing this union, is there anything else you want to say?"

In unison, Cooran and Sephina recite, "Yes, we, Cooran and Sephina, now invite and welcome Jah to join, guide, protect, complete, and sustain our union."

With this, King Rohaan proclaims, "May Jah bless your union."

Then Cooran holds Sephina's face in his hands and kisses her passionately on her lips for the very first time. The crowd roars with joy, cheers, and claps with great delight. Cooran and Sephina turn to face their guests and bow. They then sit down on the throne with

King Rohaan, as the ceremony comes to an end and the celebration begins.

Each tribe and territory give beautiful and exotic presentations of music, dances, gifts, and all sorts of treasures to the royal couple. The celebration continues for many hours into the night, with feasting and dancing.

After many hours of more celebrating—eating, dancing several times, and greeting their guests—Cooran and Sephina retreat from the crowd. There is to be a special chamber prepared for them, but, Sephina takes Cooran by the hand and leads him to her own chamber.

As they stand before the doorway of her chamber, she squeezes his hands and says, "I, Sephina, wife of Cooran, now invite you, Cooran, husband of mine, to my chamber." He gently kisses and then lifts her, carrying her into her chamber. They enter to see the chamber beautifully decorated with ribbons and flowers, also filled with candles, and wonderfully aromatic with incense.

As is the custom, Cooran and Sephina have three months to celebrate their union. During this time, they travel to several of the most beautiful and interesting territories and neighboring kingdoms Cooran thinks Sephina will admire. They enjoy their ventures together. She is now able to meet some of the people and see some of the places he regularly visits for his work. She also gets a glimpse of some of the people and places where her own work will prove beneficial in the years to come.

In the third and final month of their union celebration, Cooran and Sephina return to Daaveran to their very own palace. It is much smaller than the king's palace but grand just the same. There are at least twenty sleeping chambers: five are for the servants, five for honored guests, and one large master chamber for them together, along with separate chambers for their individual interests and others to be filled with their "little ones." Of course, there is a lovely courtyard, having one side covered and the other side open to the skies, all overlooking the river. They are both very pleased.

Once settled, they invite King Rohaan and several special guests to their new home. These special guests include Nan, Cooran's other best friend, and his wife Wanu; Jacq, Nan's father and now close friend to the king, who is accompanied by Sonji and her sister, Alexni. Sonji and Alexni are longtime friends of Jacq and his family. Jacq has been courting Sonji for almost a year now and has in recent months introduced the sisters to his friend the king. And now they meet Cooran and Sephina.

The open courtyard is chosen for a beautiful moonlit celebration. The evening is delightful with delicious foods, soft music, and refreshing breezes, culminating in pleasant, exciting, and yet exuberantly unexpected conversations.

Cooran and Sephina tell of their travels and the joy of their union. Nan and Wanu announce their expectancy of a third child. Alexni expresses her interest in Sephina's work and offers her services. Finally, Jacq declares his love for Sonji and asks her to be his wife. Sonji excitedly accepts.

From all the excitement, the atmosphere has finally settled down enough for everyone to notice a beam of light shining down over King Rohaan. Sitting in the open air of the courtyards, the moonlight's reflection on the river somehow casts a beam of light on the king. He sits with a radiant smile and a calm of peace. As everyone looks upon him, his smile grows ever greater.

He says with a chuckle, "I have great news too that I want to share with you, my family and closest friends." The king continues, "I have made a great and life changing decision, and I invite you to join me, if you so desire." Everyone practically moves to the edge of their seats, eager to hear the king's news. King Rohaan looks up to the sky and breathes deeply, still smiling radiantly.

Finally, he softly but firmly proclaims, "I have both seen and experienced the love and faithfulness of Jah for myself. I have come to find and know Him to be the one true God. Through Cooran and Sephina's wonderful examples, I am compelled to become Jah's humble and obedient servant. Therefore, I, Rohaan, King of Daaveran, now, most joyously,

*"Invite Jah to be my one true God."*

# SEED TIME AND HARVEST

## (NEW BEGINNINGS)

*O*ver several years, Cooran, and more recently Sephina, have planted seeds about the truth and love of Jah into the king's life. However, it is the king's personal encounter with Jah that has made the real difference. Even though only in recent years did King Rohaan learn of this foreign god, he has now come to acknowledge Jah as the one true and living God. King Rohaan is experiencing for himself Jah's goodness (His favor and the abundant crops) and unconditional love (the significance of his dreams and Jah's plan to save his kingdom), which brought him to the decision to trust and serve Jah as his own God.

The king, just the night before, conveyed to some of his family and closest friends his thanks and appreciation to Jah and his decision to worship Him only and live forever under His authority. Of course, Cooran and Sephina were elated to learn of this decision. A few of their friends were happy for him as well, while others were respectfully indifferent.

Early this morning, in this vast and colorful kingdom, the great King Rohaan is awakened by the soft sunrays caressing his face, as they break through the cracks of his chamber windows. He jumps out of bed, slowly stretches, and then strolls out onto his balcony.

He breathes in deeply and proclaims, "How beautiful a day it is I have been granted to see! The sun has never been brighter, nor the sky clearer." He draws another deep breath and walks down the few steps leading to the courtyard area overlooking this, his kingdom of Daaveran.

He sees the beauty of the village below and the fields of many crops to his right and also in the far distance to his left. He knows of the great number of beasts grazing in the fields beyond where his eyes can see. The king relishes the vastness of his kingdom and the territories he commands. He sees the extremely abundant crops soon to be harvested and acknowledges that it is all far beyond his control. Never has he witnessed such abundance. This he can only attribute to Jah.

He pauses to consider the greatness of the new foreign God he has recently learned of and now chosen to serve. The king remembers how he scoffed and thought, *What mighty gods would have concern for mere man?* and had once deemed it simply foolishness to consider any possibility of there being only one true God. Now, King Rohaan can only give overflowing thanks to this God, Jah, for extending favor upon him, his people, and his kingdom.

This year's crops are from the first year of the special harvest foretold to the king. Though he was already convinced, King Rohaan has been anxiously waiting to prove to himself and others whether Sephina's interpretation of his dreams will prove true or not, which will, in turn, either validate or refute Jah's plan. This year's crops have not yet been harvested, but there is undeniable evidence of a grander and more viable yield than any year he has ever witnessed, in either quantity or quality.

King Rohaan knows the greatness of his own power and authority as king, but he also recognizes his limitations. He finds the thought of a limitless God who cares for all His creation quite refreshing. By contrast, his own ancestors considered anyone not of royal blood as their inferior subjects. Many of his ancestors thought themselves to be gods and had little regard for those outside the royal family and even less for their servants. Because of their brutality and disregard for the lives of slaves and common people, as well as the greed and selfishness displayed among the royal courtiers that he himself witnessed before his rule, King Rohaan vowed inwardly to be a different kind of king.

At first, he was destined to adopt the same cruel ways and rulership. However, when he was a boy of not yet fourteen, his very life was saved from drowning. A strong young slave saw the young prince's plight and rescued him from the deadly waters. As others ran along the river's bank, the slave kept the prince above the surface. Then the torrent began to push them into large rocks. At one point, the slave's body took a mighty blow as he tried to protect the prince. Though badly injured, the slave was determined to hold on to the young prince. The current eventually brought them to shallower and calmer waters, where the young prince was then able to pull the slave from the water. The slave died as a result of his rescue of the young prince. But before the slave took his last breath, he asked Prince Rohaan, "Please show kindness to my people, as I have shown you."

Prince Rohaan recognized this slave as one he had harassed and humiliated mercilessly for several years. The prince's actions were mainly because this slave seemed to emit joy and kindness, despite his position in life. The young prince never had the opportunity to ask this slave for forgiveness but vowed that, from that time on, he would show respect and kindness to others, no matter who they were.

As the king continues to ponder his trust and commitment to his newfound God, he realizes that though he has shown kindness over many years like the young slave, he has never really experienced the joy he now feels. This sense of joy is unlike any happiness he has had in times past—when he met and married Cooran's mother, when Cooran was born, or again when he and Cooran were reunited. This new happiness seems to come from within, a pure joy welling up from the heart. With these thoughts, King Rohaan now recognizes why this ordinary day seems so extraordinarily beautiful and vibrant. He is also amazed at how differently he feels and sees things, even in the short time since his declaration to serve Jah.

Still in the courtyard, looking out over his kingdom, King Rohaan dances and shouts with great joy, "Thank You, Jah, for Your goodness to me and my kingdom! You are the one true God, and I will now serve You, as long as I have breath!"

Later this same day, the king is visited by Cooran and Sephina. They enjoy a light lunch, as they speak more of King Rohaan's decision to serve Jah. The king expresses his amazement at how Jah shows him and his people such favor, even though they are not yet His followers. The king tells the couple, "I must decree that everyone shall follow and serve Jah, the one true and living God."

Sephina expresses to the king how noble this gesture is but tells him how Jah desires that each person choose to serve Him for themselves. "Jah will not and cannot be forced on anyone," she tells the king.

King Rohaan ponders for a while and agrees. Then he says, "I so want my people to experience this joy and freedom I am enjoying. What can I do? I am their king, so they must do as I command."

Cooran reminds him, "Father, do you not remember how resistant you were about accepting a foreign god, even from me, your own son? It is only natural to reject the unknown. Consider the many years of this kingdom's strong beliefs and culture of serving kings, the royal family, and the many ancestral and ceremonial gods."

King Rohaan ponders as Cooran continues, "As with you, your citizens may have to experience and recognize Jah's goodness for themselves in order for them to acknowledge His existence and accept Him as their God."

Cooran and Sephina suggest that the king should remind the kingdom of Daaveran that it is Jah who is providing them with the great harvests in preparation for the difficult years ahead. They say to King Rohaan, "Let the people know that Jah is the one true God who is not only providing for and protecting them but loves them and also wants to be their God. The choice will be their own. And with your permission, as we go into the territories, we will plant seeds of this message of Jah's love to all who will hear."

The king agrees. Soon he sends a "Proclamation of Jah's Goodness, Love, and Provision" to his kingdom and territories. With like minds and hearts, King Rohaan, Cooran, and Sephina grow ever closer in their relationship with each other. As time goes on, other family members, friends, servants, and slaves accept Jah as their God, but not everyone. Though slavery is not abolished, it is now unlawful to abuse slaves. This law does not go over well with some slave owners, but they obey, since the slave owners themselves can now be sold as slaves as their punishment.

As everyone goes about their lives, King Rohaan daily thanks Jah for His goodness. Cooran and Sephina share Jah's love as they perform their tasks, going to and from villages and territories. They also tell those willing to hear of Jah's truth and His desire for them to know Him. "Jah is a good God, and He loves you!" they tell them.

Finally, the time to harvest the crops has come. After all the plowing, the planting of seeds, and months of care, it is now time to enjoy the first fruits of their labor. Sephina, her friend Alexni, the many workers, and even the animals all labor diligently to bring in the first harvest. Oh, how abundant are the yields from the many fields planted and cared for through the seasons. Numerous workers are cutting the grain with their sickles, and many are binding the harvest with papyrus ropes, while other workers and animals carry bushels of wheat and baskets of corn and other produce to their designated areas. Some of the harvest is processed for immediate use, and the rest is stored against future needs.

It is quite amazing to see it all come together. All that is taking place in the kingdom of Daaveran is being duplicated in two other areas in the king's territories. The past month seem almost a blur. How busy, tiring, and yet exciting it all is. Sephina sighs with joy, for the first year's seed time and harvesting have finally come to a successful end.

As she looks over the harvested field, she says, "Jah, You have provided us with great and rich blessings, this, our first year of plenty." She breathes deeply and exclaims, spinning in a dance, "Thank You, Jah! You are an awesome God!"

The following days are celebratory all over the whole kingdom and territories, rejoicing over the abundant harvest. Never before has anyone ever seen such great yield from a harvest. This is truly the first of the seven good years before the seven years of famine. After the many months of supervision, the first major phase of The Great Harvest Plan has come to its final stage, the first year's bountiful harvest.

Sephina now plans to relax awhile. Cooran will soon be returning from his trip of two long weeks. Oh, how she misses him, even though she has had very little time of her own to think. She now welcomes the extra day she has before Cooran is to return home. She rests and pampers herself in excited preparation for his return. She knows that Cooran himself will be tired and worn from his long travels.

The following day, she makes sure fresh flowers are cut and placed around the palace. There is hot water for a long, relaxing bath awaiting the prince's arrival. Fruits and fresh bread accompany some of the freshly harvested produce to add to the delicious meal being prepared. The aroma of succulent duck fills the air. Sephina checks everything herself, one time over, to make sure all is perfectly in place.

It is noised in the palace that finally Prince Cooran has arrived. He is dusty and looks very tired. Even so, he arrives with a big smile, as Sephina eagerly awaits his entrance into the palace gates. She runs to meet him as soon as the gates open. As they meet, he embraces her, lifting her as he spins her around. Then he gives her a big kiss and says with great enthusiasm, "Congratulations, Sephina! Everything looks wonderful." He continues, "I saw that the fields have all been harvested. You've done it!"

Sephina smiles and thanks him. Then she tells him tenderly, "I really missed you." Cooran holds her close, telling her how he missed her as well, and then kisses her passionately. She takes him by the hand, leads him into the palace, and softly exclaims, "Welcome home!" Cooran takes in the beauty of the colorful flowers all around and breathes in deeply the aromas of the much-anticipated meal to come; but first he indulges in his hot bath and most appreciated pampering. He and Sephina enjoy their delicious meal in the courtyard, admiring the beauty of the setting sun over the river.

Later, they stroll under starry skies, snuggled arm-in-arm. Cooran tells of his trip, with nothing new to report—except, he says with enthusiasm, "You would be so delighted how your instructions to Jah's plans are being carried out throughout the territories. Everything has worked perfectly."

As they stop to sit, he turns to face her and softly says, "I'm so proud of you, Sephina." He then cuddles her face with both hands and kisses her softly on her forehead.

Sephina tells him proudly yet humbly, "Jah and I make a great team!" Then she smiles with pure joy.

As they sit, she begins to tell him how everything has come together. She admits that it's been hard work. She starts to reminisce about the planting of the first seeds; watching the rich, green sprouts begin to show over large stretches of land; colorful fields of various produce; then the tall, golden stocks of corn, barley, and wheat waving in the gentle breezes. How wonderful it all was.

"Is not the handiwork of our God just amazing?" she says, beaming with delight. Cooran nods in agreement, drinking in her words, the sounds, and the very presence of his beautiful bride. They have several days to relax from any tasks or pending duties, so they continue to enjoy each other's company.

One late evening while stargazing from the courtyard, Prince Cooran tells Sephina, holding her close, "I am so thankful to Jah for choosing me for you. It is my joy to be one with you."

Looking deep into his eyes, she replies, "You are my strong protector, my respected lord, my gentle and loving king, and my best friend. I do love you." She caresses his face, then kisses him deeply. On that very night, a special seed of their love is planted.

$\mathbf{B}$ack to work, Sephina is now coordinating the separation of grains, whether for current consumption or for future distribution. All the processing of the grains for storage is now complete. Large compartmental structures, called granaries, have already been constructed to house each type of grain harvested. Builders have also constructed numerous above-ground cisterns of different sizes throughout the land. These cisterns are to catch water, as the rainy season will bring heavy downpours of water upon the kingdom. They are all properly prepared and readied for their designed purpose.

A great number of domestic felines are employed to help protect against possible unwanted visitors—more specifically, rodents. One major task will be guarding the stored goods from citizens who do not heed the warnings of the coming famine and may become desperate or hostile. Soldiers are being trained specifically for this purpose, with rules and guidelines based on the severity of a perpetrator's actions.

This first year's yield is so substantial that Jah's plan now looks more realistic to Alexni and the other supervisors with whom Sephina has shared this information. Sephina herself has no doubt: "If Jah said it, it can be fully trusted." The plan is to use this first year's abundant crops toward the first four good years. Sephina has no doubt that the following six years' yield will be just as good as this year's, if not better. The plan for the harvest distribution of the remaining six great "years of plenty" is as follows:

> _Year Two (of Harvest Yield)_ ~ *fifth through*
>       *seventh good years*
> *(anticipation of population growth included)*

*Year Three (of Harvest Yield)* ~ *first and*
    *second bad years*
*(includes a small number of foreign nations*
    *first and second years)*
*Year Four (of Harvest Yield)* ~ *third and*
    *fourth bad years*
*(larger number of foreign nations' third year)*
*Year Five (of Harvest Yield)* ~ *fifth bad year*
*(greater number of foreign nations' fourth*
    *and fifth years)*
*Year Six (of Harvest Yield)* ~ *sixth and most*
    *of final famine year*
*(sixth year for foreign nations)*
*Year Seven (of Harvest Yield)* ~ *remainder of*
    *famine year and following year for recovery*
    *from famine*
*(seventh and recovery years for foreign nations)*

Sephina knows that even though King Rohaan has shared the news of the coming famine with rulers of neighboring kingdoms, many think the king and his dreams foolish. Severe famines are nothing new to these nations—but "Seven years? That could never be" is their response. Though the prediction of the seven abundant years will prove true, Sephina suspects that these nations will consume the yields with little to no regard to the predicted seven years of famine. To mention some strange God and His plan is simply outrageous to many.

Fortunately, some have listened. For those farther beyond her reach and know nothing of the coming destruction, Sephina prepares for an overflow of foreigners coming to Daaveran for their food supplies. Amazingly, Jah has made her aware of things she would have never considered. With that, her thoughts drifts to her family. She prays and thanks Jah, trusting Him to take care of her family by providing for their needs, especially during the time of famine.

While finalizing her week's work, Sephina just has to exclaim to Alexni and the workers nearby, "My Jah is so wise!" She smiles widely. "Isn't He just amazing?" The workers smile and nod affirmatively.

Then Alexni says, in evident awe, "Sephina, I am dumbfounded at how amazing your Jah is." She continues, "I had some doubts about your plan becoming fully possible, but this harvest has proven greater—far beyond my greatest expectation. Yes, your Jah is ... is truly amazing." They all laugh as they take their leave toward homes and families.

Several weeks pass, and Sephina notices some changes taking place. However, these changes are within ... within her body, to be exact. One evening, shortly after discovering the cause of these changes, she has a special meal prepared for her evening with Cooran. She is so excited about her news, she's not sure she can wait until the dessert to tell him.

Cooran comes in from working at the palace with his father all day. With the king's birthday quickly approaching, several judicial cases need review for final judgment. The task is tedious. So the king and the prince take some time to clear their heads by sparring with each other. Shortly after they start, they are joined by King Rohaan's two younger sons, Sooran and Timri. They also practice their javelin throwing. It is all rough, tough, and sweaty man's play.

Now Cooran is glad to be home, in the tender care of his loving wife. He holds her in his arms and notices a strange sparkle in her eyes. He is curious, but Sephina tells him with a broad smile, "You will have to wait until after dinner."

"So let's eat!" says Cooran with a big grin.

"Not before your bath, we won't!" Sephina retorts, leading him by the hand, while jokingly holding her nose. They laugh and chat until and then throughout their evening meal.

"It is now after dinner," Cooran says excitedly. With that announcement, dessert is served to Cooran first. It is a single seeded date. Dates are one of his favorite fruits, but pitted and by the handful. So Cooran looks at the date, then at the servant serving him, back to the date, and then at Sephina, with a puzzled expression. She only smiles, nibbling on the bowl of grapes that is placed before her.

Finally, he asks, confused but with a smile, "Sephina, what is the meaning of this?" He continues, "Just one date—and it still has the seed? I am puzzled."

"Yes!" Sephina says with a smirky smile and a stiff tone of voice. "There were many seeds planted this past season. They have produced an abundance of fruits which we can now enjoy." Cooran shook his head in agreement, but still puzzled.

She goes on, "But you my husband, have planted a single seed, which I now carry." Cooran looks at her, wide-eyed with excitement.

"Yes, Cooran! I am with child," she says delightedly. He leaps up from the table to her side, picks her up, and hugs, kisses, and spins her around with more kisses. He is so thrilled that tears flood his eyes.

When Cooran finally speaks, he softly tells Sephina, "What a wonderful team you and I make." It is a joyous evening, but that single un-pitted date languishes forgotten in its dish.

The following day, Cooran is anxious to tell his father. But he agrees with Sephina to wait and surprise the king with the news on his birthday. With only a short week before him, he still struggles with some of the judgments he is to make as part of King Rohaan's birthday ritual. He prays and asks Jah for wisdom, as he has many times before.

Finally, he receives a peace within about his judgments and recognizes Jah's guidance. He says quietly, "Jah, it is so good to know that You are always here for me and that Your judgments and guidance are always just and true. Thank You, Jah!"

At King Rohaan's birthday rituals, Cooran's judgments are unanimously accepted and praised. Cooran acknowledges his Helper and says, "To Jah be all the praises, for He is truth." He is glad it is all over and the time of celebration has come. He and Sephina stand on either side of the king's throne, as the dancing, greetings, and festivities continue.

After gifts are presented to the king and the three have a quiet moment to themselves, Cooran presents Sephina as their gift to the king. The king looks puzzled, but only for a moment. Sephina motions, as if cradling and then, rocking a baby in her arms. King Rohaan slowly rises from his throne and hugs them together with great delight.

A few weeks later, Cooran and Sephina's meet at their palace with intimate friends for a light meal. As is their newly established custom, they will meet at least once during each new season. During this time, they plan to share what new thing is taking place in their lives or just simply enjoy their friendships.

This evening, Cooran's old mentor, Jacq, is beaming with his new wife of three months, Sonji. They tell of their new life together. Nan and Wanu talk of the struggles and the joys of having three young children. Alexni tells of her amazement at the wonders she has witnessed about the reality of Jah and His abundant provisions produced from this year's special harvest. The king has nothing new to report but announces that he was given a very special birthday surprise. He beams with excitement as Sephina and Cooran share their good news. Everyone expresses great joy and congratulations.

Weeks and months quickly pass, as Sephina sees her body transform to accommodate the new life growing inside her. Cooran continues his work throughout the territories, but she must delegate more and more of her duties the closer she comes to her time to deliver. She considers this her personal harvest time. In the meantime, the kingdom and territories enjoy the produce of their first great harvest.

As her time to give birth draws near, Sephina notices a growing anxiety. At times, it seems to overwhelm her, and Cooran is unable to settle her fears. They decide to pray together, holding hands. Then he pulls her close and holds her tenderly in his arms.

He prays over her, "My loving Jah, thank You for being the good and wonderful God that You are. As You know, Sephina has become anxious, struggling with fears as she prepares to bring forth our firstborn. Please, give her peace. Let her know that You are here with her, and that no harm will come to either her or our child. Help me too, to be strong for both of us. Thank You, Jah, for answering our requests."

Even after his prayers, Cooran encourages Sephina to seek Jah's wisdom. He himself inquires of Jah and discovers that his wife's anxiety comes from her dealing with her own mother's death in childbirth. He presents this revelation to Sephina and then prays again with her. Shortly thereafter, Sephina finds peace and a renewed excitement to bring forth their firstborn.

At last the day comes, but Cooran is feverishly striving toward his return from his services of one of the kingdom's nearby territories. He has been unexpectedly delayed for several days, finalizing a judgment over a civil dispute between two family tribes. Now Cooran's chariot is driving hard and fast, as he knows that Sephina's time is near.

However, he did make prior arrangements, in the unlikely event he is not there on time. Cooran knows that his father will make certain that Sephina is well cared for. Cooran had to encourage his father also, that everything would go well with Sephina. He and the king prayed against the fears and anxiety Sephina experienced earlier. Cooran noticed his father's subtle hesitation at first. He was reminded that King Rohaan also experienced the death of Cooran's own mother, after she gave birth to him.

Finally, the time has come. King Rohaan is close at hand, since Cooran has not yet arrived. Sephina labors for several hours. Within minutes after Cooran's arrival in the palace, the soft cries of their baby come forth. Cooran runs to Sephina's side. He gently caresses her hand and softly kisses her forehead.

The midwife gives him the bundle that is their firstborn. As Sephina sits up, Cooran lifts their little bundle upward and prays. "Jah, we give You great thanks for our beautiful baby girl, Maneisha."

Sephina nods in agreement and says out loud, "Jah, the seed You have blessed us with has now come forth. We are truly a family, and there is no fear of the coming famine."

She continues,

*"Thank You, Jah, for she is our greatest harvest!"*

# FA ~ MI ~ NE ~ LY

## (FAMINE + FAMILY = FAMINELY)

$I$n this great land of Daaveran, the royal family is now welcoming their newest member, Maneisha. A girl child, she is the firstborn to Princess Sephina and Prince Cooran. She is joyously welcomed by her parents and her grandfather, King Rohaan. Now, with a growing family, the king rejoices to see and hold his first grandchild. With the kingdom of Daaveran experiencing its greatest harvest ever, Cooran and Sephina recognize Maneisha as the most precious of the great yields that Jah has provided them. For these great blessings, Jah is highly honored and praised by this royal family.

As King Rohaan looks at the little bundle he holds, he exclaims with delight to the proud parents, "How beautiful a child she is!"

A smiling Prince Cooran agrees with the king's evaluation. "So you see what a great team Jah, Sephina, and I make?" King Rohaan chuckles and proudly beams, as other family members now come to welcome little Maneisha.

Each day, Sephina marvels at the wonders of Jah's awesomeness. She takes notice of the unique and intricate makeup of her little Maneisha—everything so tiny and yet so perfect. She thinks out loud and expresses, "What an awesome God You are, Jah! And I give thanks to You for Your goodness."

$D$ays stretch into weeks, weeks into months, and months into just over a year. Maneisha is becoming more beautiful and ever so delightful. She has stolen her father's heart. Cooran helps Sephina with Maneisha in many ways whenever he is able. He makes sure to spend time with her; always tender, yet firm when necessary. Oh, how Maneisha loves her father.

Even so, Cooran's love grows ever deeper for Sephina. His continued gentleness and love for her gives her reason to ponder. She realizes how she appreciates Cooran loving her so much, for: he is quick to forgive and apologize, yet is very slow to accuse and never condemns. He seems always willing to communicate in both good times and bad; he is patient, tender, and kind in both speech and deeds. He is protecting, caring for, and providing for their family. He listens and takes time to walk and talk with her, loving her even when she seems unlovable. And he desires her for who she is rather than simply needing her for what she can give.

But most important, Sephina recognizes how Cooran continues to grow in his love for Jah, as well as his obedience and submission to Him. She has learned herself how trusting better enables one to more readily obey. She observes that the stronger his trust in Jah grows, the quicker he is willing to obey Jah's instructions. Cooran's obedience to Jah strengthens his commitment to his family—loving her unconditionally, above his love for himself; and making her second only to Jah in his love and priorities. And for this, Sephina joyfully respects and loves him that much more, showing him the same respect she has for Jah, no matter the circumstance.

Sephina acknowledges within herself that Cooran is not perfect, but neither is she. They have had disagreements and even argued. Yet she loves and is totally committed to him, striving to reciprocate the courtesies he showers upon her. She concludes, after deep reflection, that Cooran possesses many essential qualities that contribute to the success of their union. She believes that these are the qualities that all maidens should look for in a potential mate. However, she knows that such qualities are greatly enhanced by and are a direct reflection of a man's deep relationship with Jah. Again, Sephina truly thanks Jah for His wonderful gift of Cooran as her husband.

Whenever she has an opportunity, she expresses to the unwed maidens she encounters how and why they should wait and preserve themselves for the husband Jah has for them. She even gives requested advice to those already in a union.

At a previously planned gathering, after putting Maneisha down for a nap, Sephina meets with a dozen invited unwed maidens. They have all gathered for a light lunch and fellowship. These maidens include Cooran's two sisters, several assistants from Sephina's workplace, and five who are currently serving in her home (employed only until they choose to move on to something better for themselves, though some stay out of loyalty and appreciation). Three of the servants were prisoners along with Sephina who have recently been released or pardoned. The two younger servants— former slaves needing jobs, whose freedom Sephina purchased— are also new to her staff. Each of these maidens has expressed either an interest in following Jah, a desire to one day marry, or both.

After the maidens have settled in under the covering of the outdoor courtyard, Sephina welcomes each of them. She then prays, "Thank You, Jah, for this beautiful day and for this delicious meal You have provided for us. May You bless each of these precious maidens and our time together, as we learn from You and seek to grow in knowledge and wisdom."

Then she has the maidens introduce themselves to each other. The air is quickly filled with chatter as they go around to get acquainted. Two of the former prisoners, Symir and Tokimi, and a younger servant, Nia, are a bit reserved and awkward to be interacting with those of a higher social status than their own. Yet they participate.

Sephina's friend and assistant, Alexni, is a bit standoffish at first, for the opposite reason, but she too participates. They all settle once again as the food is served, and they begin to feast on pheasant and harvested produce. Once the maidens have finished their meal, Sephina begins to share some words of wisdom.

They each seem excited for this opportunity to ask questions concerning such matters of the heart, though Symir, Tokimi, and Nia are still a bit reserved. Then, Cooran's sisters, Eisha and

Nashtah, and several others of Sephina's assistants, Maida, Jada, and Brosis—all followers of Jah—notice and purposely begin to socialize with them, making them feel more at ease. Sephina excitedly wants to address such matters of interest, especially relationships. She silently prays to Jah for His guidance to properly instruct and provide wise answers to these maidens.

She first asks them to ponder the idea of self-love and to rate how they value themselves. Sadly, most rate themselves rather low, including some of her assistants and several followers of Jah. She then tells them, "I'd like to start by telling you how important it is to love yourself in order to have healthy relationships with others. This is especially true regarding your relationship with Jah or a mate."

Maida asks, "Isn't that being rather prideful and selfish?"

Sephina answers, "It can be. But if you have a healthy love for yourself, you are able to treat others as you'd like to be treated: with respect, compassion, and forgiveness. Even if others do mistreat you, your worth does not depend on the actions of others. Also, loving yourself enables you to develop confidence in who you are. You can then look for opportunities to help others, rather than focusing on your own inadequacies and needs."

The other assistant, Lerum, speaks up. "I've seen many who clearly love themselves act selfishly and even cruelly toward others."

Sephina tells them, "This is where knowing Jah is important. You first must understand how valuable you are to Jah and know that His love for you is unconditional. Receiving Jah's unconditional love and value for you and others will help each of us love and value ourselves and others equally. Also, we will find that He is quick to forgive us when we are wrong and ask His forgiveness. This alone should lead us to show appreciation to Jah, develop and keep a humble attitude, and pass forward such goodness as acceptance and forgiveness on to others."

She adds, "Some who seem to love themselves and are yet cruel to others tend to have experienced deep hurts or abuse. They hide their hurts behind a disguise of self-importance and self-centeredness. They usually have difficulties loving themselves, yet want to be loved by others. However, they repel others by their haughty and selfish attitudes, directing their self-hatred onto others. Ultimately, they are needing to receive the love and healing only Jah can give them. Purposely, Jah uses His followers to be His hands and feet, in order to express His love and healing to those who are lost, hurting, and needy, as well as to those who are simply His.

"Every one of you is beautiful in the eyes of Jah," she continues. "When you don't feel or believe that you are beautiful, know that true beauty comes from within—having love, patience, and forgiveness for yourself and for others. It is only the evil one who tells us the lies that we're worthless, unlovable and inadequate. Reject such lies. Start by forgiving yourself for your past, and let Jah heal you with His love; then trust Jah to guide you each day, and always allow Him to protect your future by obeying Him."

One of her servants, Deena, asks, "Why would Jah value or even love a servant or a slave?"

Sephina tells them, first directing her answer to Deena and then to all, "Because Jah is Creator of all mankind (lads and maidens), and He sees each as equal—none having greater or lesser value (slave, servant, or free) than any other. His unconditional love lets us know that we cannot earn or destroy His love for us by our words or deeds or any other way."

Nia, the more reserved servant, seems a bit agitated. "If Jah already loves me, why do I not feel His love? Where is the evidence of His love?"

Sephina responds gently, "Though Jah's love is limitless, many of the benefits of His love are conditional. One such benefit is sensing His presence. Such benefits require that we first choose to become His child, loving and serving Jah as our God, in order to receive all the benefits of His love. For He will not force Himself upon anyone. Yet Jah greatly desires a relationship with each of us."

Sephina excitedly continues, first looking at Nia, "However, there is wonderful evidence of the unconditional benefits of His love for us"—now looking all around with a warm smile—"like our very ability to give and receive love; the sunshine and rain, all earth's beauties; our abilities to think, reason, learn, speak, and create; our health, strength, breath, and life itself; and much more."

As Sephina closes the first part of their time together, sweet treats and fruits are served, giving the maidens time to ponder what they've just heard. Then as they eat, Sephina tells them of the many great qualities that she loves about Cooran. She also tells how she must always express her love for him through respect, appreciation, and encouragement. She says, "Our words are powerful. We must use them to help build up and never to tear down our mate or anyone else."

As the discussion continues, there are more questions.

Zeerah, the third former prison-mate and a bold believer in Jah, shyly asks a pointed question: "What happens when you do not have the option to choose your mate?"

Sephina understands her point. "My best advice would be the same for those who do have a choice. First, pray, asking Jah's to help you become the best mate you can be and to give you the ability to love your mate unconditionally. Seek out his best character traits, and encourage those hidden treasures within him. Wisely discourage the unwanted traits, and try to overlook them when you are able or when you must. Then ask Jah to orchestrate and bless your union so that it brings Him glory as He guides you.

"Though the choice may not be your own, and he may not seem to be the right mate at first, through your obedience to Jah and Jah's love for him, your 'unchosen' mate may become better than one you would have chosen for yourself. Even so, as you trust Jah with your life—and He may allow (but will never create nor cause) an undesirable or even an evil situation—He promises to protect and be with you, no matter your circumstance."

Sephina goes on to tell them some of her history: where she came from, what she endured, how Jah has never failed her, and where He has brought her. She then explains, "Loving and serving Jah does not mean that life will always be easy and without challenges. Quite the contrary in many cases. Even if your mate turns out to be cruel and unlovable, Jah can use your love and forgiveness to turn your husband's heart toward Him. Yet each person chooses the character he or she wants to possess, either to follow Jah or to remain easily susceptible to the evil one's influence. However, Jah promises to be with you wherever you go. As you are obedient to Him and trust Him, He will work all things out for your good."

Sephina continues, "Jah requires that we too must love others unconditionally, be quick to forgive even if we are wronged, and trust that Jah's heart is for our best. For no matter the abuse we endure or the wrong we suffer, we must receive Jah's healing. For only His healing gives us the ability to truly forgive and love those who abuse or wrong us. Otherwise, we remain victims, filled with bitterness and unforgiveness, rather than the victorious ones Jah wants delivered and freed."

Sephina promises the maidens, from her own experience, that Jah is both trustworthy and faithful. She then explains that developing a healthy relationship with Jah will bring them to a place of maturity in their lives, their hearts, and their attitudes. This alone will enhance the success of their union, if they do marry, as well as all their other relationships.

She continues, "And if you do have a choice, choose a man who loves Jah above all else. The more he grows in obedience to Jah, the more he will love and care for you and your family. Do not choose solely on the basis of a man's form or outer strength or wealth, but look for a man with substance of character and inner beauty."

And then with a chuckle she says, "Now if you have a choice, and a lad not to your liking shows interest, be gentle and considerate of his feelings. You are not obligated to just anyone who comes along, but you don't have to be rude either. Remember that their hearts can be hurt as well, and Jah loves them too."

Sephina smiles softly. "In choosing, first consult with Jah. Be moved by your heart and not by your feelings alone—for your feelings can change as easily as the waters flow down the river." The maidens chuckle. She continues, "Choose someone you can be yourself with, laugh with; someone who wants you and you want to be wanted by him. While you seek the one your heart longs for, do consider those who cherish being with you. Among them will be the one you spend the rest of your life with, and it's best you both enjoy being with each other."

Then she cautions. "And beware of the one who pretends to have a genuine interest, only to win you over for his selfish desires or foolish pride. For once he has accomplished that goal, his true, yet undesirable self is revealed." She frowns with seriousness. "Such a deceiver is influenced by the evil one. He has no desire for a deep or future bond, only for self-gratification. When he abandons, he leaves behind much hurt, shame, regret, and disappointment. Hence the importance of seeking wise counsel, especially Jah's."

Sephina strongly encourages the maidens to respect their bodies, first to honor Jah and second to safeguard precious gifts they can present exclusively to their own husbands, by avoiding intimate bonding before marriage. She tells them how such acts outside a marital commitment cause emotional heartaches and the tearing of a spiritual bond that has formed. Even a single occurrence can lead to mistrust, disappointments, guilt, hurts, unwarranted comparisons, and unforgiveness. Still, such acts can be forgiven and healed by Jah.

She continues, "Jah wants each of us to guard our hearts and bodies, and to not give either away too easily or prematurely. He gives us such guidance not to prevent us from enjoying life, but rather to protect us from unnecessary hurts and disappointments, so that we can have true pleasure and satisfaction in living."

Then she reminds the maidens that there are no perfect men— or women either. She stresses that everyone needs to accept people for who they are, without false expectations for others to change or become someone else. No one initially possesses all desirable qualities, but as a person seeks and trusts Jah, such qualities can be attained and developed. But that choice belongs to each one, allowing Jah to transform them.

Sephina tells the maidens, "Here are Jah's major goals for joining a man and a maiden in marriage: first, that Jah Himself may be glorified as the two become one; second, that the two find joy and pleasure with each other; then, that a strong, loving, and caring family is created; and finally, that their love may be shared with others—as in Jah's family, united as one with love."

She continues, "As you know, not everyone will marry. However, by Jah's guideline, all men and women are to keep themselves pure in reverence to Him and themselves. Jah designed and reserves the intimate bonding of one man with one maiden under a lifetime commitment of a marriage covenant. Again, His guidelines are truly for our own protection and not to deprive us of pleasure."

Finally, Sephina brings their time to a close, telling them, "Above all, know that a successful union requires continuous work. So, never fail to regularly pray to Jah for your mate's best, and thank Jah for the wonderful man He has given you—especially when he's not at all lovable; make his needs and desires a priority, and be the best you can be for yourself, for Jah, and for your mate and life partner."

The maidens thank Sephina for this time, and some ask if they may regularly meet for such talks. Sephina is pleased and agrees to host these gatherings. The maidens disperse to talk and engage in separate conversations.

Then Alexni joins Sephina, who is about to pray with Nia and Symir. She apologizes for interrupting and asks if she too can join them in asking Jah to be her God. Sephina and the other maidens gladly welcome her.

Sephina first prays for these maidens and then leads in a prayer as they repeat, saying, "Dear Jah! Thank You for loving me. I now choose and ask You to be my God. I commit myself to love, to serve, and to worship You and You alone. Please come live in my heart and live through me. Help me love and forgive others also, as You love and forgive me. I surrender all that I am, all that I have, and all that I hope to become totally to You. I thank You now for becoming my one true God."

After saying this prayer, the maidens in unison seem to release a slow, deep breath, as if releasing heavy burdens. All the other maidens join them by gathering around.

Alexni exclaims as she wipes tears from her eyes, "Wow! Jah truly is an awesome God." She then hugs first Nia and Symir and then each of the others.

As the others hug, Nia blurts out, sobbing and smiling, "I can sense Jah's presence, and I can feel His love within and all around me."

Most cheer, as Sephina embraces Nia, and Sephina's other house servants come out, rejoicing.

Deena tells Nia as she starts weeping, "I am not there yet, but I am so happy for you." Then she smiles "I believe I will one-day trust Jah to be my God too."

Just before the maidens leave, Maneisha wakes from her nap, and they all get to hug her. After they have left, Sephina is delighted by the experience of such a refreshing and fulfilling day. She gives Jah thanks and then goes to relax and play with Maneisha until Cooran comes home.

**A** little over two years have now passed since Maneisha's birth, and Sephina has fully resumed her regular routine. She is coordinating the planting and harvesting of various crops for the years of plenty. Cooran is back and forth throughout the kingdom, territories, and neighboring nations, conducting civil and criminal judgments. Though both are busy in their normal duties and responsibilities, it is their priority to make and spend time together as a family—praying, playing, living, loving, and sharing. Maneisha is growing and loves playing in the courtyard with her father, who likes to toss her up into the air or spin her around by the hands as her feet rise from the ground. Oh, how fun it is to play!

Now many in the kingdom, territories, and other nations are enjoying the abundance of these great harvests, but not everyone is following the plan to preserve against the future threat of famine. Most believers in Jah heed the warnings and plant their own gardens to join the combined effort.

However, some who do not worship Jah are also following the king's lead by preserving for their future as well. Still others scoff and enjoy the years of plenty, still not believing the threat of the seven years of famine. Many foolishly think this great abundance will never end, usually giving homage and sacrifices to their own gods. Even so, Prince Cooran and the king's officials remind and warn citizens in every territory and the neighboring lands, wherever and whenever possible.

In years past, an annual feast was made to celebrate Prince Cooran's birthday. But because of the coming famine, he personally decides to forgo four of the six birthday celebrations in order to help provide for other nations. Even so, the king's birthday celebrations continue as usual. Yet nothing in excess in view of coming hard times, despite the abundant harvests.


However, this year to everyone's surprise, King Rohaan decides that as part of this year's birthday celebration, he will crown as queen the mother of his other four children. Lady Maarianette was chosen for him as his concubine, ten years after his previous queen proved unable to bear him children. It has been eight years since Queen Velmon died, and the kingdom of Daaveran has been without a queen.

Lady Maarianette has proven over the years to be goodly and honorable, a faithful and kind woman to King Rohaan, as well as to

Prince Cooran. She is truly a loving mother to the royal children. Lady Maarianette has also chosen to become a believer in Jah.

Years ago, shortly after Prince Cooran was reunited with the king, there was a grand ball for both king and prince to find their brides. Neither was found at that time. But now King Rohaan, after much prayer, counsel, and consideration, has determined it ideal to make Lady Maarianette his new queen. The king admits to himself that he always admired Lady Maarianette's gentle and humble persona. So a grand ceremony is incorporated into this year's annual birthday celebration.

But before making a decree, King Rohaan decides to first inquire into Lady Maarianette's feelings toward him. He decides to allow her to make the final decision. Of course, this is unheard of, but these options are only made known to Lady Maarianette, Prince Cooran, and Princess Sephina.

As the king has not called upon Lady Maarianette in an intimate capacity for several years, she is rather anxious when she is unexpectedly summoned before King Rohaan. Upon her arrival, the king attempts to ease her mind, as he invites her to join him for a private meal.

As Lady Maarianette meets the king on the covered balcony, she nervously bows before him. King Rohaan stands and says, "Welcome, Lady Maarianette!" He pulls out her chair and beckons her, with an awkward smile, "Please join me for dinner."

Lady Maarianette becomes less nervous as they nibble on grapes and fresh berries. King Rohaan is about to present his proposal, but just then, a light, delicious meal is served. So instead, he tells her, "Lady Maarianette, let me first start by letting you know how much I appreciate your loyalty and kindness throughout the years."

She smiles, visibly surprised. She has always sensed the king's appreciation but has never heard him verbalize it.

King Rohaan continues, as he beams with pride, "But my greatest thanks to you are for the four beautiful and well-mannered children you have given me."

Lady Maarianette herself then smiles with pride. She tells him, "My king, it is not only my duty, but my great honor."

As they chat and make small talk, Lady Maarianette becomes relaxed and more at ease, as the evening progress.

Instead of presenting the three options, King Rohaan asks, "Lady Maarianette, will you do me the honor of joining me again tomorrow night for dinner?"

Surprised again, Lady Maarianette accepts, musing about what is going on with the king. "My King, I would be delighted to join you for dinner."

The following night, King Rohaan is the one anxious, and Lady Maarianette notices and wonders why. Shortly after they have completed their meal, King Rohaan escorts Lady Maarianette to a more comfortable seating that overlooks the kingdom of Daaveran. As they settle an arm's length apart on the soft cushions, King Rohaan turns his entire body to face her. He then nervously presents his proposal, as he lifts her chin to allow her to look directly into his eyes.

He tells her, now taking her hands, "Lady Maarianette, I have both respected and admired you for a long time. However, I've found that my heart is being drawn more intimately toward you."

Taken aback by this revelation, Lady Maarianette shyly smiles, as she unconsciously drops her head. As he gently lifts her chin to look again into her eyes, King Rohaan continues with more energy, yet softly and with a smile, "However, I have a proposal I want to present to you for your consideration. Because of the delicacies of this matter, as well as my feelings toward you, I wanted to present these three options to you personally. The latter two options are unusual but are feasible."

Lady Maarianette, puzzled, looks into the king's eyes, and he tells her, "The first option is for you to remain as Lady of the Courts; the second allows you to be released from this position, in order, to pursue your own personal interests."

And then more warmly, gently squeezing her hands, he tells

her, "And third … it would give me great honor if you chose to become my wife and the queen of Daaveran."

She sits stunned as the king strongly emphasizes that the choice is solely her own and that he will honor her decision. Rather amazed, she stays silent until he reassures her that if she chooses to relinquish her position for her personal interest, he will honor her decision and provide both safe and adequate arrangements for her.

He also informs her that he will allow her several days to consider her options. Lady Maarianette leaves her evening with the king in a daze, her head spinning with bewilderment. Before she leaves, King Rohaan presents her with an exceptionally large and lovely arrangement of assorted flowers.

After she leaves, he prepares for bed after standing for a quarter hour looking out at his kingdom below, while thinking about what just took place. He hopes his words to Lady Maarianette were clear, loving, and not overbearing. He's never had cause or desire to win a woman's heart since his first love, Queen Madeline.

After retiring to bed, he is a bit restless. He gives Jah thanks that His will shall be done and finally drifts off to a restful sleep.

That night, Lady Maarianette finds it difficult to sleep as well, tossing and turning. She talks to Jah, giving Him thanks and praises until she too falls asleep. When she awakens the next morning, she has somehow convinced herself that this was all a wonderfully strange and desirable dream—but only until she turns and sees the beautiful floral arrangement.

She smiles and jumps out of bed, dancing, as she says, "Jah! You are so awesome! Only You knew my heart's desire toward the king, and now You are bringing it forth. Thank You, Jah! I do love You!"

So it does not take Lady Maarianette long to decide. However, she waits two days to prepare herself, gather her thoughts, and reflect on her readiness for the joys, challenges, and duties of accepting the king's offer to become his wife and queen. She has difficulty believing this is really happening to her. Both thrilled and astonished, she feels as if she is in a dream from which she does not want to awaken.

When Lady Maarianette finally meets with King Rohaan for dinner the third evening after their previous meal together, she unabashedly tells him, "My king, I have always thought myself rather fortunate to be the mother of the king's children and a loyal servant to a great king and a kind man. But now, to be offered the position of wife and queen ...."

She pauses and continues more softly, tenderly, and with a gentle smile, "—to a man, I have long admired and have grown to deeply love. This is greater than an impossible dream come true. So I humbly and joyously accept the king's proposal, to become your wife and your queen."

King Rohaan then kneels before her, takes her hand and kisses it gently.

For several nights following, they continue their private dinners, becoming better acquainted in their new relationship with each other. Actually King Rohaan is learning more about Lady Maarianette's history and her likes and dislikes, since she already knows much about the king.

The following week, one of their private dinners includes the three princes—Cooran (37), Sooran (22), and Timri (19); the two princesses, Eisha (20) and Nashtah (18); and Sephina (32), the king's second-in-command. This is a time to share the decision to wed with their immediate family. Both Cooran and Sephina are thrilled, for they love and are fond of Lady Maarianette. The younger princes and princesses are elated. Great excitement and congratulations greet the new royal couple, for it has never been considered before to place a lady of the courts, not of royal blood, in the position of queen.

The following day, the royal decree is made and invitations to the combined royal event—the king's birthday and his marriage to Lady Maarianette—are sent off. There are several months of preparation ahead and much excitement is in the air. The grand event takes place with attendees representing many other tribes and nations joining King Rohaan and soon-to-be-Queen Maarianette's celebration.

Now with all this joy and expansion of the royal family, Sephina's thoughts often drifts to her own family back home. She often longs to see them, despite her sisters' betrayal. She prays Jah's protection and provision for them all, especially her beloved father, as the years pass and the famine approaches.

Throughout the years, more of the royal family, along with Cooran and Sephina's friends, are accepting Jah's invitation to be their God. They too are amazed at the wonders of the abundant harvests and how the plan for their survival is so beautifully coming into place. To recognize the love and mercies of a God who prepares and provides—even for a people who neither know nor serve Him—is simply amazing and quite compelling.

In the first year, the abundance of the harvest is measured and the excess stored. Each year's harvest expands so greatly that it nearly defeats efforts to keep count. Near the close of the fifth year of abundant harvest, Sephina finds that she is carrying Cooran's and her second child.

Though very busy with their daily duties and responsibilities, the news of their new family member takes away some of the stresses they are experiencing. Sephina more readily delegates the physically strenuous tasks to others, as Cooran makes sure to shorten his travels in the latter months, as the baby's time of delivery comes closer. In the meantime, Cooran, Nan, and other traveling officials continue to warn the outer territories and other nations they visit. They tell and remind the people of the quickly approaching end of the abundant harvests and the beginning of the devastating famine of seven long years.

Back in Daaveran, Sephina finds that during this time of carrying her little one, she has not become anxious as before.

Instead, she finds herself spending time pondering the past. It is not a time of regret or self-pity, but a time of wonder at Jah's goodness. She recognizes the maturity and wisdom He has developed within her, which enable her to fully love and totally forgive: her sisters who betrayed her, the slave traders that mistreated and sold her, her mistress who falsely accused her, and her former fellow prisoner who had forgotten her. Sephina learned at an early age that, though others may fail you, Jah never will.

King Rohaan looks in amazement, as his great kingdom of Daaveran is expanding from within and from without. Many families are multiplying. The number of foreigners is increasing as commerce grows and the crops yield in abundance. There are children running about playing in the distance. Newcomers are exploring the bustling streets and settling in the nearby villages. Also there are workers in the fields, while others move about the markets.

The king finds it difficult to imagine that his now truly flourishing and vibrant kingdom could ever possibly be devastated by a famine. He realizes that if he had not been warned and even come to know Jah for himself, he too would not believe such devastation is near. He has learned not to trust in or rely on only what he once knew, believed, or even now sees; now he relies only on Jah. He never dreamed that he might possibly believe in only one god, not to mention one who is faithful and caring, as he has found Jah to be. Nor can he fathom such abundant crop yields as his kingdom and territories have known these past five years.

Though the foretold famine is only two years away, King Rohaan is confident of Jah's provision and His protection. King Rohaan cannot be more thankful to Jah for choosing to implement His plan by using the Kingdom of Daaveran. The king is proud and grateful for Sephina's hard work in coordinating and putting into place Jah's Great Harvest Plan.

As instructed by Jah and directed by Sephina, great reservoirs for water, seeds, and much grain have been constructed. These water cisterns and granaries house the excess of water and abundance of produce given through the past years. There will be seeds of all kinds, preserved for replenishing trees, plants, and produce, for use after the seven years of devastation caused by the famine.

How honored King Rohaan is to have Sephina as his second-in-command, as a member of his royal family, but especially as a fellow believer in Jah. As a fellow believer, King Rohaan can confidently seek godly wisdom and direction for himself as well as for his kingdom. He knows that he no longer needs to make decisions on his own. With Cooran and Sephina trusting Jah as well, the king has peace about the future of his kingdom, despite the famine to come. He is joyous that his new queen, others of his family, some friends and courtiers, and many citizens are now also believers in Jah. Yet, he is disappointed that many others do not believe.

As the sixth year of abundance begins, life continues with new and great wonders. The king's second son marries, and a grand celebration is held. Prince Sooran and his bride, Kevaah, are given one of the provinces already supplied with a distribution site, as a wedding gift from the king and queen. A palace also is constructed and prepared for the new couple. The royal family grows.

The king and his new bride more often spend time with each other, their children, and their grandchild, and now they look forward to having more grandchildren. They enjoy the abundance and beauty of their flourishing kingdom but remain quite aware of the famine soon to come. Their faith in Jah's great provision, now gives them greater hope rather than fear, in His caring for them in the dark days ahead.

When Sephina's time is near, Cooran makes no travel plans. He simply enjoys her special beauty as she grows with their second child. Then finally, Emily is born. Another reflection of Jah's goodness, she comes into the world with great expression of life and energy.

Maneisha is thrilled to have a little sister, as her parents rejoice in the blessing of their two beautiful daughters. However, time is growing short. There is just a little more than a year left to enjoy this land of abundance and beauty, with their children and family before the dreadful famine is to come.

Life seems to move quickly, as the last year of abundance comes and goes. And now the seven abundant years have fully passed, and the seven-year famine begins to show its ugly head. Only several months earlier, all the final harvest has been securely processed. This will be the harvest that sees them through the last year of the famine and the year of recovery to follow.

Even so, there is a very small portion, about a tenth of this last year's great harvest, set aside. It is to be used to celebrate, honor, and give thanks to Jah for His goodness through the years and signal expectancy about His faithfulness for the years to come. This great event is dubbed the Festival of Thanksgiving. It is to be grander than any of the king's annual birthday celebrations. With Sephina's strategic planning, there is no fear of shortage. But the true emphasis of this festival is a recognition of Jah for His great blessing and an expression of gratitude to Him for His love, His wisdom, His warnings, and their trust in His abundant provisions.

As for all grand celebrations in the kingdom of Daaveran, invitations are sent out to the citizens, territories, and neighboring nations. They are all invited to this great Festival of Thanksgiving. King Rohaan wants to use this event to give thanks to Jah publicly before everyone, every territory, and every neighbor and to remind them of the severity of the soon-coming famine.

Preparations are made, and the celebration takes place within weeks after the final great harvest is complete. During the opening ceremony, King Rohaan calls for the attention of all his citizens and visitors. As the crowd quiets down, he tells them, "Welcome, everyone, to our Festival of Thanksgiving. We are here to give Jah all the glory and thanks for the seven years of abundance."

There are whispers in the crowd, but the king continues, "Many of you may not acknowledge this God, Jah, but He is the reason for the great harvests we have received over the last seven years. Therefore, we want to thank Him now for His provision and in advance for His protection from the harsh seven years of famine soon to come."

Unexpectedly the crowd roars with cheers, claps, and whistles. Then a low chant begins and escalates to a loud, vigorous chant of "Thanks be to Jah!"

As the chant quiets, King Rohaan beams with delight. Then he encourages the citizens of Daaveran and their visitors saying, "We must fully trust Jah, yet we will need to use wisdom in consuming and preserving grains and water for the long road ahead."

Finally, for everyone, but especially those who have not heeded the warnings of the last seven years, King Rohaan advises, "Know that there are stored provisions available through the direction of Princess Sephina, my second-in-command. Understand also that each year the famine continues, there will be greater challenges. So as one big family, we must work together and be considerate of each other. Please be assured that everyone will have access to the available goods, and there is no need to fear a shortage."

The king does caution that these provisions will be provided at a reasonable charge. He mentions that everything is in place for peaceful, orderly, and smooth transactions, though life such as they have enjoyed for the past seven years will drastically change. "There will be a number of adjustments, partly as we expect a great number of foreigners seeking provisions. I ask you all to be patient, hospitable, and courteous to these visitors."

The king understands his responsibility at having received this warning from Jah and his obligation to open his provisions to others who have not heard the warning. Therefore, he has prepared to receive all those who come peaceably.

King Rohaan reminds his guests, "Everyone in my reach has been adequately warned of this coming famine. We offered guidance so that you too could be better prepared."

He mentions that many will be coming from faraway nations, once news of Daaveran's provisions has spread to them. He says that measures are in place at every distribution site if it becomes necessary to squelch any disorder. He makes clear that no anarchy will be tolerated, and no uprising will go unmet.

He tells them also, "My sole desire is to provide for our very large family, wherever they come from, in peace and with order."

Once the king finishes his remarks, the festivities begin, with music, dances, conversation, and presentations of every kind—acrobatic performances, animal shows, and fire displays—with much food and drink. Unlike past celebrations, this Festival of Thanksgiving lasts for three full days. It is elaborate and spectacularly colorful; it is delightful and extremely enjoyable; and it is extraordinarily abundant.

Within weeks after the grand Festival of Thanksgiving, the lush and beautiful terrain of the kingdom of Daaveran begins to show signs that the famine is about to start. The summer months are brutally hot and dry. There is no rain in sight during the rainy season. The ground is now parched, brittle, dry, brown, and lifeless. The earth and the air seem to suck everything dry. No moisture is in the air, just dust and stillness. This is only the first year, and already feelings of misery and despair are evident all around. However, there is an abundance of food and water. With this reality, many recognize that because of Jah, they have much more to be thankful for than to complain about.

Even so, it is not long before the scoffers and noncompliant citizens become fearful and desperate. They are the first and most frequent users of the distribution sites. Within the first few months of the famine's devastation, only the local scoffers and noncompliant citizens are buying the grains and water. By the end of that first year, ridiculers from Daaveran's territories and provinces, along with a few foreigners, have begun to arrive. They seem to have traveled from far and wide, seeking provisions to survive the lack caused by the famine. Many have no idea of the expected length of this famine and are grateful for the generosity of the kingdom of Daaveran in sharing its abundance.

One hot, dreary day, a group of about fifteen citizens from one of Daaveran's territories come to the distribution center. They've traveled from a province a little west of Daaveran that has concerned Cooran. He has told Sephina how both the leaders and citizens waved away warnings from Cooran and Nan, and later from others, to prepare for the famine. Now standing before Sephina are three officials of Uvandi province and a dozen of its citizens.

Onarus, Uvandi's leading official, speaks with bold desperation, after he and his citizens bow in humbled reverence before Sephina and her assistants. He tells them, "We come, humiliated by our foolish pride in disregarding your warnings. We were wrong in our arrogance and poor judgment and ask that you have mercy to forgive us. We beg you to kindly allow us to purchase provisions for our families, that we may not die."

Sephina walks down from the platform where she stands, with an assistant and two of her soldiers following closely behind her. She approaches the anxious citizens of Uvandi and then stands before Onarus.

She then graciously and lovingly speaks to him and his citizens: "Citizens of the Uvandi province, you are members of Daaveran's family, and you are always welcome here."

She warmly extends a hand of greeting to Onarus, as her assistant directs the citizens to the processing center. Onarus expresses great appreciation to Sephina and Daaveran's citizens for not turning them away, knowing of their terrible treatment toward the officials who simply came to warn them. Onarus and Uvandi's citizens give sincere apologies and are relieved to know that they can freely acquire needed provisions without being rebuffed. Soon they leave Daaveran with happy hearts and abundant supplies for their province.

As the famine drags on far beyond many citizens' limited expectations, the price of needed goods goes from mere local currency to their servitude to the king. The famine lasts so long that many lose their livelihood, use up all their earnings and savings, sell all their belongings, and even sell their children and finally themselves into servitude in order to survive.

Those who have heeded the warnings of the king and his officials fare far better for themselves and their families. Still, many do need to purchase from the king's supply. These have followed the plan as best they can by planting their own grains, saving a portion for the famine, and even saving extra monies for when their supplies run out. But because of the severity and the duration of the famine, even their means eventually run out.

As Sephina is now implementing the distribution portion of the plan Jah gave her, she observes and sees how brutal the famine has been to all. Everyone from far and near is feeling its effects, but not everyone is reacting the same. Sephina notes to herself how one's own attitude or response toward these circumstances seems to determine his destiny. So again, Sephina finds reason to be thankful to Jah. For He has taught her how to develop and to keep an attitude of gratitude, no matter what her circumstance or where in life she finds herself.

She is also thankful that during the king's presentation at the Festival of Thanksgiving, he emphasized Jah's goodness. With this emphasis on Jah's goodness, Sephina's heart is reassured of His provisions and protection for her family back home.

Sephina hopes that each citizen will recognize that, though Jah is Creator, He has given each one the ability to choose good or evil, to obey or disobey Him, and to accept and follow His plan for their life—or not. Everyone has a choice, and Jah will never force anyone to follow Him. But His desire is that everyone will trust and obey Him; otherwise the consequences of not doing so is to fall under the evil one's control.

By the midst of the second lean year, all the distribution centers see larger numbers of foreign visitors seeking provisions. However, the distribution center in the kingdom of Daaveran is the largest, receiving more visitors and foreigners from the farthest lands to the northeast. The other two centers are strategically placed, providing for the king's most distant territories to the northwest, west, and southern regions, enabling them to extend out to their neighbors further west and south of them. Sephina has delegated many tasks but still oversees the actual distribution of the grains. On occasion, she ventures to see the volume and intensity of the crowds. Though newcomers are increasing in numbers, the atmosphere remains peaceful and orderly for the most part.

However, on one such occasion, Sephina happens to notice in the distance, a seemingly large group of women approaching the distribution center where she stands. For some reason she cannot pinpoint, this group of women stirs her interest. She keeps them in her gaze. As they move closer, she gasps in recognition and delight. These women are the older ten of her eleven sisters.

Sephina immediately recognizes the wonders of Jah's goodness. Wow! Look how Jah has orchestrated His plan, to provide for her very own family during this time of famine. How great is Jah, in that He cares and provides for the things that concern those who love and trust in Him. Sephina's heart is truly grateful, for her family will be saved from this devastating famine.

**What an awesome God Jah is!**

# DREAMS FULFILLED

$T$hrough the years of trusting Jah, Sephina has learned that she will not always know what Jah is doing; nor will she understand why. However, she fully trusts that He knows and wants what is best for His people. This famine, and seeing her sisters bow before her, are evidence of dreams fulfilled.

Her sisters have traveled far from their land, through rough and dry terrains. Though tired, they marvel, as they enter the large gates of this kingdom of Daaveran, taking in the wonders of the magnificent palace in the distance ahead; the beautiful palms trees still having many green fronds, despite the famine; the markets lining both sides of the street in either direction; and the large number of people, seemingly from various tribes and nations. There are all kinds of goods to be bought, but they are here for one thing—provisions. And most of the visitors are headed in that direction—to the distribution center.

There are a lot of people, but everything seems to be moving smoothly. So the sisters muster their strength, as they pull their animals behind them. They follow the crowd to the right, down the street, until it opens to a much wider circular area. To the left, halfway around, before the street narrows again, is the distribution center. Those having already gotten provisions continue around the circled area to leave the way they first entered.

Finally, the sisters bow before this kingdom's official, ready to present their request for provisions. Here, at the larger side of the distribution center Sephina stands on the platform where the foreigners are served, with two soldiers and several constantly rotating assistants. These assistants help with translations of the various tongues; direct foreigners for payment exchange; fill requests for provisions as approved by Sephina; and help with the loading of provisions. The two soldiers are specifically assigned to protect Sephina. Others stand strategically all around.

There is a similar, yet slightly smaller, area designated for the citizens of Daaveran, with assistants assigned by Sephina. They are processing the great number of local and outside Daaveranians. There are also enough soldiers all around to dissuade any disturbances and sometimes simply keep the process flowing smoothly.

At the foreigners' area, now standing before Sephina are her sisters. Here are Ruby, the oldest, Simone, and LeVette. And look, there is Judith, looking strong and confident as always. Sephina sees Natalie, Danielle, Gabriella, and Ashley. Can this all be true or just a dream itself? Finally, there are Zebeulah and Isabel.

But where is Jasmine? Sephina strains to see Jasmine too, her only sister by her mother. But Jasmine is not here. Though this saddens her heart, Sephina is still very excited seeing her ten older sisters. Naturally, they are all much older now, but she recognizes each one of them. However, not even one of them recognizes her.

Sephina dearly wants to hug and warmly greet her sisters, but recollections of Cooran's warning many years before seem to dash her happy thoughts, as fresh as if he'd said it yesterday: "Deal wisely with your sisters." Memories of the hurt caused by their hatred, when she had shared her dreams with them, flood her thoughts. Despite the hurt, Sephina has never held any bitterness or malice toward her sisters. Though those memories are of painful times, she no longer feels their sting. She breathes deep with peace in her heart, for Jah has long since healed those wounds.

However, she can only smile as she recalls that the very same day was when she first met Cooran. On that day, he comforted her about her sisters' cruelty, but more important, he rescued her from certain death. Sephina, her father, and other family members were truly thankful to Jah for bringing Cooran across her path that day.

As her sisters now bow before her, her thoughts take her back to the first of two special dreams she had as a child and the day she told her sisters about it. How naïve she was, heedless of how her dreams of her sisters bowing before her would infuriate and belittle them. How foolish she was to think that they would recognize it, as she did, as a special dream from Jah. Back then, even she had no idea what Jah had in store for her. Now at last, after many years of not knowing the meaning of her special dreams from Jah, it unfolds clearly before her eyes.

Though her thoughts bring back memories of feeling the pain of rejection, she sees now how Jah orchestrated everything to bring her family to safety during this terrible time of famine. It's amazing how Jah can use hateful and destructive deeds influenced by the evil one and cause the results to benefit those He loves. Yet now she senses a need to test her sisters' hearts—whether they still are easily influenced by the evil one, or whether they have turned toward Jah.

Her sisters speak in their native language as she listens in. The translator relays her sisters' request for provisions. However, in the Daaveranian tongue, Sephina strongly accuses the women of being spies in her kingdom. This prompts several soldiers nearby to ready themselves to move toward this area. As the translator passes along her message, the women quickly yet respectfully deny Sephina's accusations. They explain that they are honorable women, daughters of one man, seeking only provisions for their families and themselves.

Through the translator, Sephina asks the women about any other sisters and the welfare of the father of all these women. The women tell her that they have a younger sister who is with their father. They also mention a sister that once was, but is no longer—not realizing that they are actually standing before her. Still, Sephina speaks harshly to them. She tells them that they will have to bring their younger sister back to Daaveran to prove that they truly are not spies.

By now, five soldiers have positioned themselves, one on either side, and three more behind the women and their animals. The group of ten women are told to choose one from among them to return home, while leaving the other nine there in Daaveran until she returns with the younger sister.

In the meantime, as the women come to a decision, Sephina has the group of ten women held in custody for three days. Shortly after this initial encounter, Sephina can focus on nothing other than her sisters' arrival to Daaveran. How are her father, her younger sister, Dinnie, and other family members doing? It is near the close of her day, so she leaves her post in capable hands and goes home. She is excited, yet anxious. She cannot wait to tell Cooran of the day's events. She will also seek his counsel in dealing wisely with her sisters.

When she arrives home, Cooran is in the courtyard engaged in playtime with Maneisha and Emily, in one of their many games. He looks a mess. Cooran has spent the whole day with the girls, going from one adventure or game to the other. He loves spending time with the girls, but now they have worn him out, and he is ready to call it quits.

As Sephina joins them in the open courtyard, Cooran seems to breathe a breath of relief as the girls turn and dismount and then run to greet their mother. Cooran rises from his knees, transforming himself from the princesses' horse into a loving man welcoming his beautiful wife home from a hard day of work.

After the greetings, Sephina assists the girls with their bath. Maneisha, now seven years, and Emily, at three, chatter endlessly, telling of their games and playtime with their father. Since Cooran has been away for almost three weeks, the girls are sure to make up for the time they missed being with him. Sephina smiles and giggles, as they tell of their adventures.

Once settled for the night, after baths, dinner, and a short family time with the girls, Sephina and Cooran snuggle under the dry but cool moonlit skies of the covered courtyards. They would normally walk in the open courts and enjoy the view of the beautiful landscape of Daaveran, but the devastation of the famine has made the vast panorama look like a desert wasteland. And while Cooran is thrilled to relax and have this quiet time with the woman he most adores, yet he knows that she has something weighing heavily on her mind.

Before Sephina shares what concerns her, she notices that Cooran is worn out and needs some time to just relax. He asks her about her day and what is troubling her. She reassures him that it can wait until the next day. Soon, after some small talk, they both fall asleep, nestled in each other's arms.

The next morning, just before dawn, Cooran wakes first. Surprised to find they fell asleep in the courtyard, he gently lifts Sephina, still asleep, and takes her to bed. He softly kisses her forehead, as he joins her in slumber for the next few hours, before another full day.

Once the girls' day begins, time is moving. Sephina wakes up in the same frame as when she fell asleep—with her sisters on her mind. After the girls have breakfast and are getting their daily lessons, Sephina is now ready to consult with Cooran.

Cooran wakes quite refreshed and ready for any and all challenges his day has to offer, even if he must resume his position as the princesses' "horse." Oh, how he loves his daughters. They are truly precious gifts from Jah.

Finally, Sephina and Cooran are alone, again under the canopy of the covered courtyard. Cooran, noticing that Sephina still seems to carry a heavy weight, takes Sephina's hands in his own as they sit facing each other. He asks her, "My precious love, what is troubling you so? It hurts me to see you this way."

She says, "I have great news, but it's a bit complicated."

"Really?" Cooran asks. Then his mind scrambles wildly and he asks with delight and a rather strange grin, "Would it have anything to do with an un-pitted date?"

Sephina grins back with an even bigger grin, affectionately stroking his hand, "No, my love! Rather, a matter with real complications. And I need your wise counsel."

His excitement subsides quickly. Yet she smiles as she tells him of her sister's arrival. "I have not yet revealed myself to them, seeing that they did not recognize me."

Cooran, too, is excited about this great event and then can't keep from blurting out, "Sephina! Your dreams … your mysterious dreams have been revealed." He pauses. "So where are they?"

Sephina tells him more soberly, "I had them detained until we can figure out what to do. And this is the complication that I need your wisdom and counsel on."

Both happy and distraught, Cooran can hardly believe that Sephina held on to such news until morning. He knows how she has been thanking Jah and praying for protection and provision for her father and family. Understanding the severity and devastation of this famine, she can only trust Jah to take care of them. He is surprised, yet he understands her reasoning in not revealing her identity and detaining her sisters.

She also reminds him of her guilty feeling after realizing how naive she was when sharing her dreams as a youth with her sisters. Her heart aches, even now, when reflecting on how belittling her dreams must have sounded to her older sisters, the thought that they one day would bow before her—a spoiled little child of their father's. And just the day before, they bowed without reservation, not knowing she was Sephina. Yet she feels badly that she had to detain them, but what could she do?

Though not often, there have been several instances of citizen dissidence and foreigner misconduct during the famine relief distributions. However, measures including well-established forces, have been in place since the time of the great harvests to squelch any such activities.

Neither of them expect her sisters to cause any such problems, but she needs some time to figure a way to provide for her family and determine the right time to reveal herself to them. Even more, her desire is to know of and to see her younger sister, Jasmine, and her father.

Sephina wonders if her older sisters treat Jasmine with love or with the same hatred and cruelty they showed her. And if need be, she wants to rescue Jasmine from such cruelty of their older sisters. She prays that her sisters have changed for the better over the years, but she will have to test them to see if their hearts are now yielded to Jah's love or still readily influenced by the evil one.

Cooran accompanies her as she goes to inquire of her sisters' well-being, before he goes to the palace to visit with his father. However, he stays in the background, out of their view. While at the detention facility, Sephina speaks briefly with her sisters through the translator, before starting her day at the distribution center. She continues her harsh tone of accusation in their presence. But her heart longs to rejoice in reuniting with them, after the more than two decades of their separation.

After checking that all is going smoothly at the distribution center, Sephina shortens her workday, returns home, and spends some time with the girls. She then retreats to one of her favorite places, a flower garden under the covered courtyard. She sits on a bench, shaded from the sun, pondering the situation regarding her sisters' visit. She is ecstatic to see them and longs to embrace each of them. Yet she knows that she cannot allow her emotions to rule her actions. She must listen to hear from Jah with His directives and use wisdom.

Her heart becomes heavy, and she decides to pass the following day without food as she seeks Jah's guidance. After spending time with the girls before their bedtime, Sephina and Cooran discuss the matter further. Then Cooran prays with and for her. It is not often that he sees Sephina with a heavy heart, but when he does, his heart aches too.

The next morning, she awakens bright and early—even before Cooran, the early riser. Once he and the girls are up, she greets them briefly and then retreats again to the flower garden. As she prays and seeks Jah's wisdom to analyze the situation and the ways of her sisters, Jah reveals many things to her. She understands now that, because her father showed her much love, affection, and favor, she has been better able to recognize and accept Jah as her loving and faithful God. Unfortunately, none of her older sisters ever had such attention from their father. Yet they longed to sense his love for them.

As one of the youngest of her father's children, Sephina always assumed that all her sisters before her had experienced their father's affection and attention, in the same manner as she did, while they were growing up. Even when she received her special coat, she had no idea that she was the only one of her siblings to receive such honor and recognition. She was too young to know or remember if such an honor had been bestowed upon any of her older siblings. As for Jasmine, who is much younger, Sephina was not around to see her little sister grow to become a young woman.

With such revelations from Jah, Sephina's heart aches even more for her sisters and their pain. Jah shows her that her sisters were never honored or given the same love and affection from their father as she was. Looking back, she understands now her sister's hatred, remembering the favoritism her father undeniably expressed and showered upon her. She can now recognize how her sisters would have felt the sting of her dream. It was like flaunting their father's love for her and his apparent disregard towards them.

To make matters worse, Sephina was bold enough to share a second similar dream with them. She remembers that it actually was not boldness but pride that led her to tell the second dream. Her sisters had been cruel to her, and she wanted them to be kinder to her. So she thought that telling them her special dream would help them see that she was special too. She realizes now, that was the time to apply Cooran's advice to deal wisely with her sisters—by *not* sharing that second dream of hers.

Folly of youth ... what was she thinking? Actually, Sephina recalls the excitement of purely hearing from Jah for the first times through her dreams. She thought that her sisters too had received special dreams and visions from Jah. She now realizes that her dreams were not common, but a reflection of Jah's favor toward her.

It now powerfully strikes Sephina that Jah, unlike her father, does not show favoritism but richly blesses anyone who trusts and obeys Him. Anyone who chooses can have such a relationship with Jah. Though Jah loves everyone He has created, He is drawn to those who trust in Him and are not ashamed to call Him their God. Jah takes great delight to pour His extravagant blessing and favor upon them.

Now Sephina's heart yearns more towards her sisters. She sees how the relationship of the parents, especially the father, toward their child does have a great impact on how each child relates to Jah Himself. Depriving a child of love or the simple expressions of love will likely provoke feelings of rejection, insecurity, or self-hate within that child. However, even though the child does not receive love or expression of love from the parent(s), the child is still truly loved by Jah. It may be difficult, but that child can choose to receive healing and feel true love from Jah. Love is not only consciously given; love must also be consciously received. Jah will not ever force anyone to receive His love, but His love remains readily available to all. Each person Jah made unique and is precious to His heart.

Even so, Jah emphasizes to Sephina that there comes a time in each person's life, when they must take responsibility to seek and to rightly develop their own relationship with Him for themselves. Jah is always available and able to heal past hurts and pain. Jah wants each person He created to see and receive Him as the loving Father that He is. And He desires greatly to commune and fellowship with each of His children. That is so He can richly pour out His love and blessing upon each one who trusts and obeys Him.

Jah also explicates to Sephina that the evils of this world is simply influenced by the evil one, but is dictated and carried out by man's choices and not Jah's will or desire. Though He, as Creator, has ultimate control, Jah, has given mankind the free will to make choices to do good or evil, build or destroy, and to follow and obey

Him or not. So Sephina prays that each of her sisters have found their hope in Jah and placed their trust in Him fully.

Later that evening, Sephina shares with Cooran what Jah has revealed to her. They discuss it further, and then she asks him, "What do you recommend we do?"

He suggests, "I know you're going to load them with much provision, so why not allow nine of your sisters to return to your family with as much as they can carry? And the remaining sister will be detained until the others return. It will be safer and more manageable to have the largest number traveling with such provisions."

Sephina immediately agrees. "My husband, you are such a wise man. See why I need to seek your counsel? Thank you, my love!" she tells him adoringly and then kisses him on the cheek, now feeling lighter.

He is happy to see the heaviness lift from his wife and thanks Jah once again for answering his prayers. Nevertheless, because the famine is so severe, both of them are confident that the women will have to return for provisions, whether or not they choose to return for the detained sister.

Early the next morning, Sephina goes to the detention facility with her most trusted servant, the steward of her house, Niemo. She has her sisters brought before her. She tells them, using Niemo as her translator, "I fear Jah, and for that reason, I will allow all but one of you sisters to return home with provisions for your families."

The sisters' faces show a mixture of both relief and conflict, not knowing who will be left behind.

Sephina then points to her sister Simone, selecting her as the one, to stay behind in the detention facility until the others return with Jasmine. She tells them, again through the translator, "In returning with your younger sister, you will prove that you are honest women and not spies." Then she continues, "This alone will save your lives and the lives of your families. Because the famine will last for many years to come, you will need more provisions. If you do not return, it will prove you are spies. Otherwise, you are not to return to Daaveran for provisions without your younger sister."

The ten sisters look at each other with great fear. They speak to one another with heaviness from guilt-riddled hearts. They agree between themselves that this is Jah's punishment to them for mistreating and selling Sephina years ago, even though she pleaded with them not to. As they talk among themselves, they have no idea that Sephina understands every word they say.

Sephina turns away and weeps as she hears her sisters talk among themselves. She is stunned how her sisters now interpret current events as Jah's punishment for their evil treatment of her many years ago. She wipes her tears before turning to them again and commands that Simone be bound right there before their eyes and taken back to the detention facility.

As previously instructed, Niemo is to oversee Sephina's orders to have the women's bags, including Simone's, filled with the needed goods for them and their families. Unknown to the women, each sister's silver is placed back into their sacks and extra provisions provided for their journey home. Once the sisters load their donkeys, they head home, distraught with having to leave Simone behind.

As they leave, Sephina watches them go. Her heart is saddened, but she believes she will see them again, because the famine has only just begun. Besides that, Sephina is confident that this is all part of Jah's plan to provide for her family. Once their provisions run out, they will have no place else to go but Daaveran. Sephina estimates that they are carrying enough produce to sustain them for the next four months. Soon thereafter, she will finally see her sister Jasmine. This alone brings joy to her heart. She thanks Jah and continues to entrust Him with all her concerns regarding the provision, protection, and future of her family.

Months come and go, and finally it is getting close to the time Sephina expects her sisters to return. However, days, weeks, even a full month passes beyond the date, and her sisters have not yet returned. Are they so afraid to return that they are willing to starve? No, she is certain that not even her sisters, hard-hearted or not, would allow their own families to die of hunger. With concern, not fear—for Sephina traded all her fears for total trust in Jah, when her life flashed before her eyes, while sitting in the pit where her sisters had thrown her—Sephina cries out to Jah for the protection for her sisters' return. Jah, once again, gives her peace and fills her with joy, as she gives Him praise and thanksgiving.

Days seem to rapidly flash before her eyes, as more and more foreigners are coming to Daaveran in search of provisions. Even so as she has done for the past five months, occasionally she discreetly goes to see or inquire after Simone's well-being. Still, some days are so long and tiring that she can hardly wait to get home to soak in a hot bath and then have Cooran massage her tired feet.

Then, late one cold, dusty morning, something wonderful catches Sephina's attention from the corner of her eye. It is a large group of women, tiredly dragging their donkeys and themselves toward the distribution stand. They look weatherworn and hungry. She recognizes Judith leading the group, with a young woman by her side. This has to be Jasmine! Her heart jumps for joy. Before they arrive at the stand, she instructs Niemo to take her sisters to her home and to prepare them to dine with her at noon. Sephina continues her work until it is time for her midday break. Then she excitedly leaves for home to dine with her sisters.

When the ten women arrive at Sephina's home, they are afraid. They reason among themselves that they are being set up with false charges and are destined to be enslaved. They conclude that this is all because of the silver that was erroneously placed back into their sacks during their last visit. They go to Niemo to explain how they brought the overlooked payment back, with additional silver to secure more food supplies.

Niemo reassures them that they have nothing to fear. He tells them that Jah, the God of their father, has provided for them. He explains that he is the one who placed the silver back in their sacks. He also informs them that they are to dine with his mistress, the overseer.

He then makes certain that the women have been refreshed with water, to wash away the dust from their faces and feet. He has other servants to provide fodder for their donkeys. Then finally, he tells them, "Madams, here is your sister," ushering in Simone to be reunited with the ten women. They hug and kiss her, checking to see if she is well.

Judith asks her, "Are you okay?" Simone affirmatively nods.

Then Zebeulah quietly adds with a scowl, "Did they hurt you?"

Simone tells them smiling widely, "No, I was not harmed. Instead, well cared for—considering." Then more seriously Simone asks them, looking at each one, "What took you so long to return? I was beginning to think that you had forgotten me."

LeVette embraces her with a sob, "You know we couldn't do that." This cascaded into a group hug.

After the hugs and tears, Simone asks, "How is my family?"

"Everyone is fine!" says Ashley, and they all reassure her.

Then Ruby explains how their father resisted sending Jasmine back with them. Simone clearly understands, and they all laugh as she hugs each of them one more time. Then the eleven women prepare their gifts to present to this kingdom's official—the harsh woman in charge.

Shortly thereafter, Sephina arrives at her home. She greets her girls and tells them of their dinner guests. In the dining chamber, Sephina's sisters bow before her. She greets them, using Niemo to translate. Then they present their gifts to her, which include some she favored in her youth. There are honey, some spices, and myrrh—even nuts, including pistachios and her favorite, almonds.

Sephina thanks them and asks after their well-being. She inquires of their aged father and asks if he is still living. They confirm that he is alive and well. Then they bow low before Sephina again, as a sign of respect.

She looks about to see Jasmine, her little sister. She asks them, "Is this the younger sister you told me of?"

Sephina pronounces Jah's grace upon Jasmine and then abruptly turns, leaving them. She is overwhelmed with emotions at seeing Jasmine, so she leaves to find a private place to weep. Once she subdues her emotions, she washes her face and returns to the dining chamber. She gives instructions for the food to be served.

Sephina sits at a table with her girls. Cooran is out of town, not expected to return until the following day. The servants sit at another table, which is their custom during official dining. Sephina's sisters are seated at a separate table in the order of their birth. They are amazed at this. How would anyone outside their family know the order of their birth? When the food is served to them from Sephina's table, Jasmine receives five times as much as any of the others. However, the sisters show no ill feelings. All the sisters feast, drink, and enjoy their time in the home of this kingdom's official, Sephina.

She gives instructions for the eleven women to stay at her home overnight and to leave as dawn breaks the following morning. There are to be two women to each room, and Jasmine receives a room for herself. However, Judith—who had to beg their father's permission to bring Jasmine, in order that their family might live and not starve to death—has also sworn to personally protect Jasmine and make sure she returns to him. So, Judith, determined to take no chances, humbly asks to share a room with Jasmine. Judith's request is granted without objections.

Sephina later gives instructions to Niemo, as before, regarding the provisions and returning her sisters' silver to their sacks. However, this time, he is to supply as much provision as their donkeys are able to carry. She tells him to put her personal silver drinking cup in the mouth of Jasmine's sack. As always, he obediently complies with her instructions.

As dawn breaks, the women are already on their way, journeying back home to their father and families. They gave their thanks and appreciation to Niemo for his assistance. They also asked that he pass on their appreciation to his mistress.

Yet they are only minutes outside the kingdom's gates when they hear the thunder of galloping horses. As they turn to look, a small band of horses is headed toward them, raising a cloud of dust. They look at each other, praying that whatever trouble there is lies far beyond where they stand. However, the closer the horses come, the clearer it is that they are the target, and at last the horses stop right where they were.

Thankfully, Niemo is mounted on the lead horse, but he does not look happy. All the sisters gather together as Niemo dismounts. He then asks the women, "How could you repay my mistress's kindness with evil?"

He tells them how the very cup that she drinks from, which she uses to help her discern things, has gone missing. She drank from it only the night before, and it is now nowhere to be found in the palace. "Therefore, one of you women must have it in your possession," he tells them. However, everyone denies taking anything from the palace.

Niemo then commands, "Every pack and sack is to be searched, and the guilty person is to return with me to the palace."

He directs one of the soldiers accompanying him to search each sack, from the oldest sister to the youngest. Nothing is found ... until Jasmine's sack is opened.

Ruby cries out, "O Jah, no!" as everyone gasps in horror. Each of the women tears her dress in shame. Then they all reload their donkeys and return to Daaveran.

Sephina is still at home when Judith and her ten sisters return. They all fall at Sephina's feet in humility and disgrace. They cannot believe that Jasmine took the silver cup, but they have no way to prove otherwise.

Sephina asks as Niemo translates, "Why would you commit such an evil act? Do you have no knowledge of my abilities to find out mysteries by discernment?"

Judith admits, "Mistress, we are unable to prove our innocence. So we all surrender ourselves to be your slaves."

Sephina demands, "Only the one found with the cup will remain here." She continues more softly, "There is no need for the rest of you to stay. You are free to return home in peace to your father and your families."

However, Judith immediately approaches Sephina and asks, "Please, Mistress! May I speak a word to you?"

Judith recognizes and acknowledges verbally Sephina's position as equal to King Rohaan. She explains that their father is quite old and that his very life is attached to Jasmine. She also explains that they could not return for provisions sooner, because of their father's refusal to release Jasmine in their care. It is only because of the threat of starvation that their father finally agreed that Jasmine should come. She goes on to reveal that she had to commit her own life to Jasmine's safety and that their father will die unless Jasmine returns.

So Judith begs, "Mistress, please allow me to take my sister's place as your slave." She asks for permission to pay the penalty for the wrong done against Sephina so that Jasmine may return safely to their father and that he may live on until his time comes. "Otherwise, I could not face my father without Jasmine, bearing the guilt, being the cause of, and watching my father suffer until his death."

At that moment, Sephina can no longer control her emotions. She sends everyone out from her presence, except her sisters. Then, with tear-filled eyes, she cries out loud in their native language, "Sisters, I am Sephina!" but they cannot speak for fear. She beckons them closer, as she reassures them who she is. She also tells them,

"There is no need for you to be afraid—and please don't be angry with yourselves, because all that was done is part of Jah's plan to save each of you, our father, and your families from this devastating famine."

Finally, she throws her arms around Jasmine, and Jasmine embraces her. Then she kisses all her sisters and weeps over them. They all embrace and talk, less fearful and more at ease. They stay at Sephina's home until the next day, becoming reacquainted with their long-lost sister. She introduces them to Maneisha and Emily. The girls are excited to meet their mother's sisters, yet overwhelmed by gaining so many aunts at one time. Sephina then properly introduces them to Niemo, his wife, Sasha, and the rest of her home staff.

It is nearly noon when Cooran arrives home from his travels. He is overjoyed that Sephina has reunited with all her sisters. He is able to recognize most of them, even though it has been more than twenty-five years since he first met them. The sisters reminisce with Cooran about the time he spent helping them herd and shear their sheep. Sephina and Cooran both tell the sisters their individual stories of their early days in Daaveran. They tell the story of how they were reunited. Sephina's sisters are amazed at how Jah orchestrated it all.

The news spreads throughout Daaveran. King Rohaan and his officials are all pleased to hear Sephina's good news. The next morning, King Rohaan has all sorts of carts ready for Sephina's sisters. He commands that they take them to their land in order to bring their father, their children, and their families back to Daaveran. King Rohaan promises to give them the choicest land in all Daaveran. He instructs that they need not bring their belongings, because the best that Daaveran has to offer belongs to them.

Before leaving, Sephina provides excessive provisions for their journey and adds new clothing for each of them. But for her *little* sister, Jasmine, she provides lots of silver and five sets of clothing. She also sends her father ten donkeys carrying the choicest produce and cloth that Daaveran has to offer. In addition, she sends her father ten other donkeys weighed down with grain, bread, and other provisions for his journey to Daaveran. Finally, she hugs her sisters and prays travel mercies upon them. With a smile, she instructs them not to argue on their way home.

She follows the sight of her sisters in the distance outside her palace gates until they finally disappear from view. She turns to look into Cooran's eyes as he holds her close. She is unspeakably happy to have seen and spent time with her sisters, especially Jasmine. She then shares with Cooran her prayers of thanksgiving to Jah, for granting her one of her most desired wishes—to be reunited with her family, with great expectation of seeing her father once again.

Cooran fully concurs, knowing Sephina's longing for her family. He then declares, "Jah, You are great and so worthy to be praised!"

Sephina nods in agreement. The gates close in front of them as they turn to walk toward the palace. Cooran softly tells Sephina, holding her close to his side,

**"Truly this is our dream fulfilled."**

# THE BLESSING

*I*n this great kingdom of Daaveran, as the second year of the nation's most devastating famine comes to a close, Daaveran continues to provide for its citizens and their many neighboring nations. Thanks to the great blessing of Jah's plan, as devastating as the famine is, it has claimed no lives. However, the demand on Daaveran's resources has been increasing daily. More and new foreigners from outside Daaveran's territories are coming in greater numbers each passing month, in addition to those returning.

Despite the challenges and added work the famine has brought upon everyone, Sephina makes it a priority to spend time with Cooran, their girls, the king and his family, and friends like Nan and his family. However, she longs to see her father, Jasmine, and all her family come to Daaveran. It has been several months now since her eleven sisters left for home, only to pack up and return to Daaveran with their families, livestock, and all their possessions. She eagerly looks forward to their return. She knows that Jah will keep them safe, and she trusts Him to bring even their aged father to her in Daaveran. With joy and excitement for what Jah is bringing to pass, she gives Him much thanksgiving and praise.

As another year comes around, it is now time again to celebrate King Rohaan's birthday. Because this is the third celebration since the famine began, the king decides on a smaller, more intimate celebration. Only the leaders of his territories and other nations will be invited this year. His reasoning for this downscaling is not the lack of resources, for there is no lack, but the expectation of another special event. This year will mark the tenth anniversary of Prince Cooran's and Princess Sephina's union. He wants their celebration to be the grandest Daaveran has ever seen—with the possible exception of the Festival of Thanksgiving in honor of Jah, which lasted three whole days.

Even so, King Rohaan's birthday celebration is quite festive, with hopes to reassure and encourage leaders of his territories and other nations that Jah will see them through the remaining years of this destructive famine. He knows that some leaders, domestic and foreign alike, may see him as flaunting his good fortune. Still, the king would prefer them to see his celebration as sharing his blessing. King Rohaan reminds himself that he has nothing to feel guilty about, since he strongly encouraged and warned his citizens and leaders of other nations of the famine in advance. He has long warned and advised how to prepare themselves, but many thought him foolish with his dreams and warnings.

Needless to say, the celebration is colorful. Not only is this the king's birthday celebration, but it is also the anniversary celebration of the king's union with his queen, Maarianette. It has been five years since their union, and he has been enjoying every moment of it. They have shared long walks, longer talks, grandparenting, heartaches, mistakes, joys, laughter, and learning together how to hear from, follow, and trust Jah as their one true God. The king reflects about the enjoyable adventure it has all been.

King Rohaan once thought he would never again experience such love for another woman, after he lost Cooran's mother. Maarianette has been a blessing to him, and he prays that he has blessed her as well. With Jah at the center of their lives, King Rohaan could wish for nothing more.

No sooner has one celebration ended that planning begins for the next grand event. Cooran's birthday and the anniversary of his and Sephina's union is a mere three months away. The king insists that this event will be grander than any that have come before.

Cooran has chosen to bypass several years of his birthday celebrations to make sure there is provision enough during the famine for some of the smaller foreign nations. However, Jah provides more than enough with His plan. They have learned that there is no lack with Jah. So this year, Prince Cooran is excited to celebrate the ten years of his union with Sephina. Beyond that, he plans to give Sephina a grand celebration with her family in attendance. He is not sure when they will arrive, but he strongly believes that Jah will have them there in time for this grand event.

Just two weeks before the grand event, Cooran and Nan travel outside of Daaveran to several of its northeastern territories. This will be Cooran's last assignment outside Daaveran until after the grand celebration. As is their responsibility, they regularly visit territories and neighboring nations to make sure all is well there and to keep peace with the neighbors. As they journey, they see individuals and various people, citizens and foreigners alike, traveling to and from Daaveran. This has become commonplace since shortly after the famine hit, except that the numbers of people are growing each day. Even in the distance, they can see moving shapes on the horizon, bands great and small.

As Nan is about to comment to Cooran about Sephina's great achievement, one of the soldiers riding ahead of them calls their attention to a conversation with a passing foreigner. This visitor tells the soldier of an unusual sight. He says that just a day's travel behind him, he encountered a band of people, animals, and carts all moving southwestwardly toward Daaveran. He explains that this band is so large that it's like a small nation on the move.

Cooran gasps with excitement. Could this be Sephina's family finally arriving? It has to be. Nan joins him in giving thanks to Jah for His faithfulness. Cooran then orders the same soldier to return to Daaveran to give Sephina the good news. He is so excited, he wants to turn toward home, but he must complete his duties before the great event.

Sephina is at the distribution center when Cooran's soldier arrives, with the news of her family sighted in the distance. Her mind races with excitement. She orders the soldier to prepare himself to take a team with him to escort her family to the uninhabited territory called Pleesan. After working preoccupied for several more hours, she leaves for home to tell the girls and her staff the good news. Maneisha and Emily, as well as all the servants, are excited as well. She begins preparing herself to meet her family and instructs Niemo to make her chariot ready for their journey early the next morning.

Shortly after giving her instructions to Niemo, to her surprise, two soldiers arrive bringing her sister Judith and her two sons to Sephina's home. Sephina runs to greet them with open arms and tears in her eyes. Judith introduces her sons, Dante and Kofi, and explains, "Our father sent me ahead to get directions."

Sephina tells her that a team has already been dispatched to escort them to their new dwelling place. She invites Judith and her sons to refresh themselves from the heat and dust of their long journey. Maneisha and Emily, remembering Judith, bombard her with excited questions about their family and their journey to Daaveran. It doesn't take very long for them to warm up to Dante and Kofi.

Early the next morning, Niemo takes both Sephina and Judith in the chariot to meet with their family. Dante and Kofi accompany one of the soldiers in another chariot. Sephina is so excited, she refuses to contain it. She is smiling from ear-to-ear, looking from Judith to the horizon, hoping to see her family in the distance. The chariot ride is too noisy for conversations, so the women instead focus on steadying themselves during this fast, rough, dusty ride.

Sephina continues to search the horizon, smiling widely as she occasionally looks across at Judith holding on for dear life. As they get closer to Pleesan, Sephina can see the dust clouds stirring. Her large family, all their animals, livestock, and carts with all their belongings, are moving into their place of refuge for the duration of this devastating famine.

Finally, Sephina's father, her brother and sisters, and their families have arrived. As the chariot comes closer, Sephina surveys the commotion, trying to locate her father. Seeing an elderly figure, she motions to Niemo to approach him. He brings the chariot close to an elderly man with long, gray hair flowing down from his face to his waist who is leaning on a staff.

Niemo assists both women in dismounting from the chariot. Sephina runs with open arms to embrace her father. Her eyes overflow with tears of joy, and she holds him tightly. Neither she nor her father wants to let go. They examine each other, hug and kiss, and hug some more. Sephina screams at the top of her voice and proclaims, "What an awesome God we serve!" There are cheers, smiles, tears, laughter, and celebrations all around.

Jacobee is overjoyed at seeing his beloved princess, now truly a full-grown and beautiful Princess. He gives praises to Jah for letting him see Sephina once again. He beams with pride and joy.

Sephina then greets each of her sisters, their husbands, and families. Then there is Dinnie, Sephina's older and only brother, who once upon a time seemed to be almost invisible in the sea of so many sisters. He is closest in age to Sephina, and she remembers him as the little runt in comparison to the older, strong-willed sisters, though he was always her protector and friend. However, he is now tall, strong, and able to hold his own. Many more hugs and kisses pass between Sephina and her large family.

During the months of a seemingly long wait for her family to arrive, at least twenty homes had been erected for immediate occupancy. There are materials provided for temporary and new construction and for further expansion of the existing structures as desired. LeVette, Simone, and Judith begin to assign living quarters, as LeVette's husband, Mark, directs those responsible, where to lead and care for the animals and cattle. Dinnie instructs the men where the temporary housing is to be set up and delegates those responsible for each task. Natalie, Gabriella, and Isabel look to where and how they will prepare their first meal in their new dwelling place. As each person gets busy with their task at hand, Sephina speaks to her father, Jasmine, and four other sisters. She explains that she will present them before King Rohaan in the early evening.

As she tells the rest of her family her plans, the soldiers assist her father and sisters onto one of the carts King Rohaan sent to bring their father to Daaveran. After Judith's brief description of the wild ride she had, Jasmine chooses to ride in the chariot with Niemo. The rest of the family stays behind, settling into their new dwelling place, which they have now learned is call Pleesan. Sephina rides on the cart with her father and three other sisters, Danielle, Ashley, and Zebeulah, as Ruby decides to join Jasmine in the chariot. However, the pace of the chariot is a bit slower, as it leads the cart back to Daaveran. Dinnie rides with the soldier in the second chariot.

The escort soldiers accompany the chariots and cart to Sephina's home. At the palace, Maneisha and Emily eagerly await their arrival. The servants have a delicious midday meal prepared, baths readied, and fresh clean clothing and shoes awaiting Sephina and her special guests.

Upon their arrival, they are warmly greeted by Sasha and the rest of the household. Sephina excitedly introduces Jacobee and Dinnie for the first time to her daughters and staff. The girls eagerly welcome their mother's sisters and brother but are quite shy to meet the strange old man with hair everywhere. They have never encountered such a sight.

Finally, Sephina prods them to welcome their grandfather to their home. "Maneisha! Emily! Greet your grandfather—my own father."

Both girls hug their grandfather warmly. Then Emily bravely asks, "May I touch your face? The hairs are so long."

Jacobee smiles and affirmatively nods, as Sephina's shock slowly abates. Maneisha joins in to touch the leathery-faced old man and his long, gray hair. They both giggle when Jacobee twitches his mouth to make his beard move around.

Now, standing before King Rohaan, Queen Maarianette, their courtiers, and top officials, proudly Sephina introduces her father. "My King, my Queen, and this great assembly, I am so excited for you to meet my father, Jacobee."

Smiling with delight, she continues, "And this is my brother, Dinnie, and five of my eleven sisters."

Sephina points to each of her sisters as she calls their name. "This is Jasmine, the youngest; Ruby, the oldest; Danielle, Ashley, and Zebeulah."

King Rohaan descends from his throne and warmly welcomes them. He personally greets Jacobee with a strong embrace. Then he addresses Dinnie and Sephina's five sisters, inquiring, "What is your occupation?"

Ruby, as the oldest, speaks as Sephina had instructed: "Your servants are shepherds, as was our father and our father's father. We have come to live here because the famine is so severe in our land of Bronaeh."

Then Dinnie chimes in, "Our flocks have no pastures for grazing. So we humbly ask that you let us, we your servants, settle in Pleesan."

King Rohaan joyously proclaims, "I gladly present to Jacobee and his clan Daaveran's best land, Pleesan."

King Rohaan then offers that any of Jacobee's clan with special skills may come manage his own livestock. He expresses his great appreciation for all that Sephina has done in his kingdom of Daaveran. Jacobee smiles with pride and love for his daughter. King Rohaan then turns to ask him, "How old are you sir?"

Jacobee tells the king, "The days of my pilgrimage are one hundred and thirty years." He then adds that his journey has been a difficult one.

The king once again embraces Jacobee with a big smile. He welcomes and invites all Sephina's family to make themselves at home in his prized land of Pleesan for as long as they need and desire.

Jacobee then prays a prayer of blessing over King Rohaan. "Jah, I thank You for this mighty, yet kind king, who has welcomed me and my family to his home, during this time of great need. Continue to bless King Rohaan and all that is his. May You expand his territories and give favor to his name."

They all give praise and thanks to Jah for His wonderful blessing. The evening ends with a small feast and talks of the journey to Daaveran. Jacobee presents a small token of his appreciation to King Rohaan and Queen Maarianette: gifts of honey, nuts, and spices he brought from his homeland.


As the grand event draws closer. Cooran and Nan have returned to Daaveran. Cooran has reunited with Sephina's family and been able to meet and visit all the new members since his last encounter with the family.

He and Dinnie become reacquainted from many years ago, when Cooran first met him, trying to survive in an ocean of too many strong-willed women. Though Dinnie is the only son, their father favored only his younger sister Sephina, whom Dinnie was closest to in both age and relations. Cooran and Dinnie quickly bond.

The night before the grand event, Cooran and Sephina host her father, Jacobee; Jasmine and Toran, her husband; Ruby and her husband, Sumel; and Dinnie and his wife, Urma. Judith sends her two granddaughters, Tarel and Amerie, along to be with Maneisha and Emily. Just before everyone gathers, Sephina has a short visit with the women, Jasmine, Ruby, and Urma, showing them her gown and getting their opinion. Sephina takes this opportunity to give Ruby a special gift of appreciation for Ruby's attempts in times past to protect her. Though short, this bonding time is precious to the three sisters.

As they all gather, Sephina and Cooran tell more of how they were reunited and stories of the great wonders Jah has blessed them with. Sephina's sisters, brother, and father give brief highlights of their lives while separated from Sephina. Cooran tells how he came to trust Jah with his very life. They continue their talk and enjoy their evening together, retiring early in preparation for the next day's big event.

The day of the grand event is now here. Cooran's prayer has been answered, and Sephina's family is in Daaveran to celebrate with them. All Sephina's siblings want to participate somehow, to show their thanks and appreciation for Sephina's forgiveness and for welcoming them to Daaveran. Many carts and chariots are provided to transport the small nation of Jacobee from Pleesan to Daaveran.

After the beautifully orchestrated birthday and anniversary ceremony and all other activities, but just before the great feast, Sephina's family provides a delightful presentation. The women and maidens perform a memorable dance, as the men and lads express their musical talents on various instruments. To Sephina's pure surprise and delight, Maneisha and Emily take part in this dance. The performance is unlike any Daaveran has ever experienced or witnessed. This performance is a heart-touching love story of Jacobee's parents expressed through music, dance, and a bit of verbal narrative. It brings fond memories, joy, and tears to Sephina's heart and eyes. King Rohaan is truly delighted, and many guests clap their hands with grand appreciation and approval.

The feast following includes a great variety of meats, drinks, produce, breads, sweets, and treats. Many indulge in foods never seen nor enjoyed before. Others delight in delicacies offered only during such special occasions. Everyone seems to find this event especially unique and filled with an atmosphere of appreciation for the special couple, Cooran and Sephina. Jacobee and his family are overwhelmed with the ceremony, presentations, activities, and great feast, but they are especially delighted to honor and to see both Cooran and their precious Sephina highly appreciated by so many others. What a delightful time everyone has. Sephina and Cooran could not be more pleased and fulfilled. They welcome the start of their next ten years together.

The famine continues for the next five years and grows more severe with each passing year. Also increasing are the clashes with citizens who chose not to heed the warnings of King Rohaan many years earlier. However, every uprising is addressed quickly and effectively to keep peace and order in the lands. Because of the length and severity of the famine, the whole of Daaveran, its territories, and neighboring nations, would have wasted away, with no food or water except what Sephina has planned and saved as directed by Jah. Therefore, Sephina collects all the monies for King Rohaan that is found in Daaveran, its territories, and all surrounding nations. Once the monies of Daaveran's citizens are used up buying provisions, the citizens begin to sell their livestock, their homes, and their land in exchange for food and water.

Now, in the latter years of the famine, with nothing else to sell, trade, or exchange, more and more citizens are selling themselves into servitude to the king, in order to have provisions for their families and themselves. For citizens who did heed King Rohaan's warnings, Sephina is able to provide them with the very land they sold to the king, with seeds and water. This is one of the processes to provide more food and to continue to sustain life, peace, and productivity for the citizens of Daaveran. Before the famine comes to an end, King Rohaan owns everything in Daaveran and its territories, except the portion of land that has been allocated to the priests of Daaveran.

The last five years of famine have been harsh and difficult, but Sephina considers herself truly blessed that her father and all her family are near, all accounted for and well taken care of. Cooran sees himself as blessed, especially now that Sephina is at peace, having her family near in one of Daaveran's territories. King Rohaan knows he is blessed, being favored by Jah as the food source and distribution center for the citizens of his kingdom and neighboring nations. He feels extremely blessed to be entrusted with such great responsibility and to see how his obedience to Jah has helped save many lives. Even so, King Rohaan longs to see the end of this brutal famine.

During these years of famine, many of Daaveran's citizens and foreigners alike, even many who scoffed years earlier, give praises to Jah for providing a plan to counteract this devastating famine. Still, there are others who continue to scoff at the idea of one true God, yet recognize their good fortune to be alive, due to the food source provided by King Rohaan. Along with the king's warning, plans were offered to help curtail some of their dependency on the king's food supply. However, those who did not adhere to the king's warnings were the first to require food from the distribution centers within the first year of the famine. Some of these same citizens tend to be the biggest disruptors to the peace in Daaveran. They hate having now become servants to the very king who forewarned them of the length and severity of this famine. Now, their indebtedness has led them into full servitude to the king.

One such person was once a prominent citizen of Daaveran. It was discovered that he was in silent opposition to King Rohaan's praises and exaltation of a foreign god. He and his family acknowledged and accepted the benefits provided by this God, Jah, but not to the point of serving or worshiping Him. At first, his disapproval was occasionally mentioned among a circle of his closest friends. As time went on, that circle began to grow, drawn mainly from those loyal to their own ancestral and ceremonial gods. These citizens banded together in small protests against the worship of the foreign God, Jah. This protest ultimately led to outright defiance after the famine was in full force. It was discovered that Paninear, the captain of the guard, was the hidden leader behind this defiant band. Because he did not take heed to the king's warning or instructions, his many lush fields of great crops became a wasteland within the first year of the famine.

Paninear, who felt bound by guilt to Delfar because of his attempt to take a second wife, allowed her bitterness and jealousy to strongly influence him. Paninear then became antagonistic toward King Rohaan after the king had released Cooran—Norac at the time—from prison after seemingly humiliating Paninear in an attempt to rescue his own slave, Myra, now known as Sephina. When Norac was discovered to be the king's son, Cooran, the ranks of authority in the kingdom's rulership shifted, but not in Paninear's favor.

When King Rohaan had his strange dreams interpreted by Myra, Paninear's wife suggested they heed the warnings, considering them valid. Delfar reminded him how their own fields and household prospered during the time Myra was with them. But Paninear's heart had become hard with lust for power and full of pride, and he refused to hear any of it. The final insult came when his former slave, Sephina, was released from prison, only to outrank him in a position much higher than his own. This rubbed salt into an already deep, oozing wound. And Sephina had the audacity to extend her forgiveness and pardon for the wrong he and Delfar had inflicted by wrongly accusing and imprisoning her. Who asked her for her forgiveness?

As the famine has grown worse, so have Paninear and his band of troublemakers. He has eventually lost his position as captain of the guards because of his leading and influencing an uprising in Daaveran during a time when the king called for peace and cooperation. Paninear and Delfar have also lost their home and land to King Rohaan to pay for the food and water they require for survival. And because of attempts to steal provisions and destroy the granaries, Paninear and many from his band were imprisoned. Delfar and several of their family members have become servants themselves to survive through the end of the famine.

Despite the dry and ugly terrain, most citizens and foreigners are thankful for the food and water source at the distribution centers and have made the best of life. Needless to say, everyone looks forward to the end of the famine. Sephina and Cooran still make occasions to have different family members and friends visit their home once every season. It gives them all an opportunity to relax with conversation and catch up with each other's lives since their last visit.

Sephina can now include her father and invites other family members. This has all been refreshing and enlightening. However, sometimes things grow awkward when one of her sisters feels guilt rising for the wrong inflicted upon Sephina. As Sephina hosts a weekend with just her sisters and Urma, while Cooran is traveling, it is Zebeulah who gets hysterically upset. After a delicious and filling meal, the sisters sit under the covered courtyard talking of a variety of things.

Then Sephina declares, "I am ever so grateful to have each of you here. I have prayed to Jah and even dreamed of having such moments like these with you, my precious sisters."

Most of the sisters express their thanks for her having them and are also happy to lovingly interact as one big family. Then suddenly Zebeulah blurts out, sobbing loudly, "Sephina, how can you love us—love *me*—after I was so cruel and hateful to you? How can you forgive us for what we did to you?"

Everyone is shocked and uneasy. Yet Sephina goes over to Zebeulah to comfort her. She gently wraps her arms around her sobbing sister. Then she looks in her eyes and tells her, "Zebeulah, that is all in the past. Please don't cry."

Then Sephina looks around, wanting to reassure her sisters. She says, "Sisters, know that every wrong done to me, Jah has used and is still using to bring about His plan." She reminds them, as evidence of this truth, that all their families are provided for and are safe during this very long season of famine.

Then she smiles and asks, "Where would we all be now, if you hadn't sold me?" She laughs. "Besides, we might have been forced to cook each other to survive, and you may have started with me. So I am rather happy you sold me instead."

They all chuckle as Sephina begins to laugh even louder. She is the first to lighten the mood with love and reassurance of forgiveness, asking them to put away and leave those memories as relics of the past. As she hugs each of her sisters, she tells them, "Sisters, I truly love you and have forgiven you. Please receive these as my gifts to you."

It is always interesting to see Sephina's two families, of her old life and her current life, interact. Though strong-willed, many of her sisters display signs of insecurity. Sephina believes this stems from their strained relationship with their father from years past. She learns that following Jah, but not fully trusting in Him, can lead to fear, mistrust, and disobedience—excluding oneself from many of Jah's blessings. She prays that they allow Jah to heal their hearts and draw them closer to Himself. Sephina loves each of her sisters and Dinnie too and has come to respect and admire each for their unique and special traits. She therefore looks forward to each season's gathering. Cooran tells her how he too enjoys these special times with family and friends.

At another occasion, Cooran and Sephina gather with only King Rohaan, Queen Maarianette, Jacobee, and Dinnie. Having outlived his four wives, Jacobee is usually accompanied by Dinnie as his strong right hand and support. Jacobee does most of the talking, relating his life's story and the goodness of Jah, as King Rohaan asks many questions of him.

During this small, intimate event, Jacobee confesses, "I once believed that Jah's blessing had left me."

Incredulous, the king asks, "What caused you to believe that, Jacobee?"

Jacobee explains, "This is the time when I thought I had lost Sephina forever."

He tells how Jah had seen him through many difficult times and blessed him miraculously on numerous occasions. And when Jah had granted him a child he desperately prayed for, he was assured by promises of great things to come. Even Sephina's dreams, though mysterious and unexplainable, Jacobee saw as signs and a reminder. "I could not understand losing Sephina, especially sensing that Jah had great things in store for her life."

Dinnie interjects, "After seeing Sephina's coat all torn apart and bloodied, Father could not be comforted."

Queen Maarianette then tenderly adds, "Oh, that had to be hard to accept. I can't imagine losing a child in that manner."

King Rohaan asks, "Did you not consult Jah?"

Jacobee ponders and then says, "My heart was too heavy, and I believed Jah had abandoned me. Though I knew better, yet I felt He was punishing me."

Cooran is curious. "Punishing you? Why would you feel that Jah would punish you? Did you not assure Sephina that Jah's love is unconditional?"

"Yes, Jah's love is unconditional, but our wrongdoing usually has consequences," Jacobee tells them. He continues, "At that time, I had recently come to acknowledge, through talks with Sephina, that I had been unfair toward all my children. I did not impart the truth and goodness of Jah through my words or my deeds, until Sephina came. When she was born, I was much older by then and a bit wiser. But then not even Jasmine benefited much, for I was too distraught to even try after losing Sephina."

He goes on, "From our talk, I also realized that I did not value them individually or collectively as precious gifts from Jah, the way I valued Sephina. I caused division and hatred. In this, I was unfair to Sephina as well, because of the favoritism I poured upon her, exalting her above all my other children and in turn belittling them. This caused each of them great pain, resulting in their dislike for Sephina."

Jacobee heaves a deep sigh. "I had refused to acknowledge what I was doing, even though Jah had already convicted my heart. Then Sephina confronted me. We talked the day before I sent her on that journey. She asked me to stop putting her above the others, and I promised her that I would. I asked her to forgive me, and she did."

"Then days later, her sisters returned with her torn and bloodied coat." Tears fill his eyes. "It was too late, I thought. And listening to the lies of the evil one, rather than consulting Jah, I believed I had to suffer for my wrongdoing by losing Sephina."

Then with a joyful smile, yet as his tears continue to flow, he says, "But now I see and know that Jah's blessing never dies but lives on, even when His works are hidden behind the scenes. The evil that was done was not Jah's doing but the evil one's. And I suffered needlessly because I did not seek Jah's counsel."

He tells them that he also learned how people must trust Jah for themselves and for each one's family, despite what the circumstances suggest. He declares that Jah's blessing is activated by one's trust in Him. Although one's doubts and disobedience sometimes hinder and may delay the arrival of Jah's blessing, they can never destroy it.

Their talk continues, and the evening ends with everyone feeling the warmth of Jah's love for each of them and their families. Knowing of Jah's faithfulness gives them great peace and the assurance of great blessings for their future.

Finally, one day at the distribution center, several months after quietly celebrating their fifteenth anniversary, Cooran comes to escort Sephina home after a long day's work. As they ride to their home in the chariot, a light gust of wind begins to blow. Then suddenly, a dark cloud shadows the ground. There is a drop of water, then two, then four, and then many more. Cooran stops the chariot. He and Sephina look at each other with wide smiles. The raindrops fall, signaling that the famine has come to an end.

Sephina jumps from her seat to embrace Cooran as the rain begins to pour. The dry, dusty ground swallows each drop as quickly as it lands. Cooran takes the reins of the chariot once again, and with Sephina now standing beside him, he drives with more vigor.

By the time they reach their palace, they are both drenched. Niemo greets them at the gate. They find the rest of their staff and their girls dancing with delight because of the rain. Everyone is thrilled, for the water level in their rivers and cisterns has noticeably lowered.

After warm baths, dinner, and family time, everyone gathers together to give Jah thanks for bringing them safely through this long and treacherous famine. Everyone enjoys their night's sleep, with the sound of raindrops falling throughout the night.

The next morning, the sun is shining brightly. The ground is dry and parched, looking as it did for the past seven years. Even so, the famine is finally over. There is a refreshing feel in the air. Sephina goes to the distribution center as she does each morning. Today, she begins to implement plans to start rebuilding and restoring the kingdom of Daaveran after its seven years of famine. Though their food and water supplies have dwindled to their lowest points, they have sufficient supplies to carry them through another full year, even with other nations seeking grains. Jah has truly been faithful through His provisions and through His Great Harvest Plan. The kingdom of Daaveran has gone through the worst known famine and survived. Not only has it survived, but it thrives with excess, to be a blessing to many other nations.

King Rohaan summons Sephina, Cooran, and his top officials. First, all rejoice that the famine has come to an end. The king begins by giving thanks to Jah for providing for them and keeping them safe. During their meeting, the rains begin to fall again, and everyone cheers.

King Rohaan decrees another grand celebration of thanksgiving to Jah for His faithfulness and great blessing upon the kingdom of Daaveran: A Great Feast of Blessing. Again, he wants to invite all citizens, territories, and neighboring nations. This great event the king wants to commence shortly after the first harvest of the new crops are gathered. The courtiers will have a little more than a year to plan and prepare for the biggest feast the kingdom of Daaveran has ever seen. Everyone is excited and looking forward to this great celebration.

After meeting with the king as the rain has ceased, Cooran and Sephina decide to visit Pleesan to see how the Jacobee clan is doing. The sun has since dried up what little water the thirsty ground has not absorbed. So the ride is a dusty one, but with a slight cooling breeze. Upon their arrival, they find everyone gathering into a building constructed for the family's meals. They have completed their morning tasks and are gathering for their midday meal.

As their chariot arrives, someone shouts, "Welcome, welcome! Praise to Jah, the famine has ended!"

They are delighted to have Cooran and Sephina join them. Sephina is so excited about the rains and acknowledging the end of the famine, she has forgotten about eating. Once with her family and the aroma of all the familiar foods of her youth, she is ready to indulge. Cooran has no reservations when it comes to eating and takes delight in bonding with Dinnie and the many men among the Jacobee clan.

Sephina greets her father with a great big smile and a gentle hug. She asks him, "Father, how are you this fine day?"

As Jacobee embraces his beloved daughter, he says, "We have come to the end of our roughest day. Praise Jah for His many blessings."

Then Sephina goes around the meeting room testing whether she has mastered the names of all her newest family members. From her last visit, she remembers the names of four young maidens. She points as she calls, "Elizabeth, Ruhamah, Victoria, and Rebecca."

As the maidens laugh and confirm, Sephina turns to the six lads across from them. "And you are Ephraim, Aaron, Matthew, Jonathan, Tariq, and Justin."

The older lads shake their heads. Then little Justin blurts out as he runs to hug her, "Hi Ants Phina!" Those who hear him roar with laughter.

She finds that each visit she gets closer to her goal, only to have more names of the newest babies added to the family. What great blessings from Jah! She realizes that with the continued expansion of her family, she may never meet her goal, but she will continue to try just the same.

As Sephina begins rebuilding and restoring the fields toward a new harvest, she looks forward to seeing the dry, ugly terrain return to the lush, beautiful, green, and colorful landscape she adored during The Great Harvest. She is not sure if the landscape will ever be quite as rich and beautiful as it was then, but for the current dry and parched scenery to have some color will be wonderful.

During another visit to Pleesan, as Sephina is in an assembly of many of the families, she tells them of the plans for the Great Feast of Blessing. She discusses some of the details and what she is looking forward to. "I am hoping to see flowers blooming, with birds singing. And one grand highlight of the Great Feast of Blessing must include your special dancing and music."

Then Natalie chimes in, "Sephina, we will only dance if you join us."

Then the room breaks out in cheers of agreement to encourage her to join the women in the dance. With a big smile, she excitedly replies, "I'd love to!"

She happily decides to practice with the women and maidens in Pleesan and her daughters, in order to participate in a dance of praise and thanksgiving to Jah. Everyone cheers again, and she notes how great it feels to be invited and included by her sisters.

After the first new crops are harvested, all is in place for the special event. Daaveran is once again filled with life, revealing a green and colorful landscape. The rolling hills reflect freshly harvested grains. The sun is shining brightly and benignly. The air is crisp, clean, and aromatic with life—not dry, dusty, and dead. How thankful everyone is to see and know that the years of famine are behind them.

Now, for the Great Feast of Blessing to honor Jah, many homes in Daaveran and its territories are decorated with flowers and colorful banners. These banners express the citizens' personal thanks to Jah, King Rohaan, and Sephina. However, some citizens choose to give thanks to their own deity.

Each territory will have its own festivities on the first day of a three-day event. The second day allows for travel to the kingdom of Daaveran, where they join all other territories and visiting nations. As for the kingdom of Daaveran, the first day of the Great Feast of Blessing to honor Jah begins at the smaller palace of Prince Cooran and Princess Sephina. A colorful procession of jugglers, singers, dancers, music, exotic animals, and the like will parade through the streets of Daaveran. The parade is to culminate at the grand palace of King Rohaan and Queen Maarianette.

The full three-day event is colorful, filled with joy, food and drink, and thanksgiving and exalted praise to Jah. Sephina believes that Jah is well pleased—even with her attempts to praise Him through her dancing. That alone may have given Jah reason to chuckle with delight.

The years after the famine are filled with new adventures, growth, and development of the Kingdom of Daaveran. The families of both King Rohaan and the Jacobee clan grow, but the population of Pleesan expands much faster. King Rohaan continues to rule his kingdom with kindness, wisdom, and might, always seeking Jah's directives. He restores many citizens' ownership of their land, with the stipulation that a fifth of their crops belongs to him. Most citizens are thankful for life itself, after such a famine. For many to receive their land back is an added gift.

Even Hugar, one of Paninear's and Delfar's sons, receives his and his parents' land back, because he was one of the citizens faithful to adhere to the king's warnings. Eventually, he is able to purchase freedom for Delfar and several other family members from their servitude to the king. Paninear and his band of troublemakers remain in prison until their judgment is complete. Life in Daaveran after the famine has largely returned to what it once was, although in some ways life is much better, and in other ways it is not. For the most part, the populace is at peace and enjoying life.

Thirteen years following the famine, the land is in a period of laughter, love, and a wonderful life. Sephina makes regular visits to Pleesan, especially to spend time with her aging father. Jah has blessed her with this opportunity to be with her father, so Sephina takes full advantage to enjoy such pleasures. She often carries Maneisha and Emily along. These young maidens, no longer girls, have a grand time visiting with their grandfather and the great number of family members at Pleesan. They've developed special bonds with Tarel and Amerie ever since their first meeting.

One day at work, several days before Sephina's regular visit to Pleesan, Jen and Isaiah, who are sons of Gabriella, arrive with news. Her father calls for her. When she arrives, Jacobee tells her that his life on earth is coming to an end. He makes Sephina take an oath that he will not be buried in Daaveran. Sephina promises her father that his body will be buried with his father, his mother, and his first wife Haley, just as he requests.

With Sephina's reassurance, Jacobee worships Jah for fulfilling His promises to him and blessing him far beyond his greatest hopes. Jacobee asks Jah to forgive him for once doubting His promises to make him a great nation with a land of their own. Then Jacobee gives thanks to Jah for restoring his hope through what He has accomplished through Sephina's life. Sephina now begins to visit even more frequently, knowing that time with her father is coming to a close.

Some weeks later, Sephina is now told that her father has fallen ill. She, Cooran, and their young daughters ride to Pleesan at once. Before their arrival, each from the Jacobee clan has come to see and speak with him for the last time. When he is told that Sephina has arrived, he musters what strength he has to sit up on the bed.

He speaks again of Jah's promises to him, including his clan leaving Pleesan to possess land of their own. Then he asks to see Maneisha and Emily. He lays his hands on each of their heads and bestows his blessing upon them. Jacobee grants them both full rights to his inheritance, as if they are his very own daughters. Jacobee then blesses Sephina and Cooran, her brother, and each of her sisters.

After instructing his children, Jacobee draws his feet back onto the bed and breathes his final breath. Sephina falls upon her father's face, weeping. She closes his eyes and kisses him.

As promised, after the burial preparation and the days of mourning are complete, Jacobee's body is taken to the land where his parents and his first wife are buried. Sephina earlier requests permission from King Rohaan to leave Daaveran in order to fulfill her father's dying wish. King Rohaan not only grants Sephina's request, but he, the dignitaries of his courts, and all the dignitaries of Daaveran's territories accompany Sephina, Cooran, and many representatives of Jacobee's clan. The children and the livestock are left in Pleesan. A great number of chariots and horses form a large procession honoring Jacobee, taking his body to its resting place.

After their father's death, again Sephina feels the sting of her sisters mistrusting her, despite all the love and kindness she has shown them over these past seventeen years. Yet again, even though Sephina refuses to receive the hurt and rejection, her sisters fear that she will retaliate against them for the wrong done to her.

Sephina notices, during a visit to Pleesan after their father's death, a cold chill from some of her sisters. During a second visit Sephina senses the same distancing. She then decides to invite her sisters back to the palace for some time alone. However, several of the women decline. She then asks to meet with her sisters alone right there at one of the homes.

It is Zebeulah who speaks up, as they gather alone at her home. "Sephina, several of our sisters fear that now that Father is no longer here, you will soon enslave us all."

Sephina sits down slowly, looking stunned, with a feeling of disbelief.

Quickly, Zebeulah tells her, "I have tried to convince and remind them otherwise. Knowing how much love and kindness you have shown me ... shown us all ... I told them that was not so."

Sephina rises with tear-filled eyes and thanks Zebeulah. Ruby and Judith, standing closest to her, approach and hug her. After regaining her composure, Sephina smiles as she again tries to reassure all her sisters. "Please know that my love and my forgiveness toward each of you are irrevocable. Be at peace, and know that I have no intentions to enslave any of you."

Sephina now understands how Jah feels when his children mistrust and disobey Him, when He continuously pours out His unconditional love on them. So she welcomes them all to gather around for their large sisterly group hug.

Once again, Sephina is reminded how the act of parents showing favoritism to one child over another can lead to a lasting mistrust and insecurity. However, she shows compassion to her sisters, reminding them again that Jah allowed all that happened to her. She expresses to them that everything took place under His watchful control and that He used it for His purposes. Jah's promise is to see His children through whatever evil they may encounter and to bring it to a successful end. She invites her sisters to receive Jah's love and healing and His peace and comfort for their fearful hearts.

Sephina believes that every one of her sisters now feels a little more secure and less fearful. Then, as she remembers, she reminds her sisters of Jah's promise to their father to take his people away from Daaveran to their very own land. Knowing that one day she will follow her father in death, Sephina makes a request of them. "Sisters, please promise me that you will take my bones with you to Jah's promised land when you leave Daaveran. I am entrusting you with my remains. Please do not leave me behind in this land. Let this reassure you that I have forgiven you and that you are safe with me here in Daaveran."

As she looks at each of them, they smile, promising that either they or their descendants will fulfill her request when the time comes.


$A$s life continues, Sephina and Cooran experience the joys of seeing Maneisha and Emily begin families of their own. They occasionally take trips to Pleesan to visit her large family. As a time of laughter and fun, Sephina still tries to master everyone's name.

Back in the kingdom of Daaveran, they never fail to spend time at the palace with King Rohaan and Queen Maarianette. Cooran's brothers and sisters all have families of their own now and have moved as leaders of other territories of Daaveran. On special occasions, Sephina will accompany Cooran during his travels to the other territories, where she can visit with Prince Sooran, Princess Eisha, Prince Timri, or Princess Nashtah, Cooran's siblings, and their families. However, everyone comes together for the combined annual celebration of King Rohaan's birthday and the anniversary of the king's and Queen Maarianette's union.

One late evening, shortly after the sun has set and a full moon is rising, Sephina sits in the open courtyard waiting for Cooran to join her. They plan for a quiet, relaxing time together in the soft autumn breezes. As she waits, she ponders, recognizing how blessed she truly is and always has been, since trusting Jah as her God. She sees that no matter the situation and no matter what is going on around her, because of her trust in and obedience to Jah, He always gives her the greatest victories.

She admits to herself though, that there were times when she did not feel Jah's presence with her, during some of those difficult times in prison, or when circumstances seemed to indicate that Jah was not looking out for her, like when the chief cupbearer forgot about her. But she has learned that Jah is always with her, and Jah always looks for and brings out what is best for her. So she knows not to solely rely on how she may feel or how things may appear—especially when they contradict Jah's promises to her. She knows that her ultimate hope and reliance are solely in Jah, her one true God.

Just then, Cooran comes out with two lightweight blankets thrown across his shoulder, carrying two cups of hot tea. Sephina wondered what was taking him so long to come out. Now, he comes bearing gifts. Cooran gives her both cups, then he drapes one blanket across her legs and the other across his shoulders. As he settles beside her, she then gives him both cups and covers his legs with her blanket. She leans back onto his chest and takes the two cups again as Cooran draws his blanket around her shoulders. She turns slightly to give him a smile, a cup, and a soft kiss on his chin, just before tasting her tea.

Sephina nestles back and begins to reflect on Jah's timing. Sometimes it can be disturbingly long. But oh! the rewards for patience and endurance. She was encouraged as a child to dream big, and dream she did. But never did she fathom what challenges, adventures, and fulfillment her life might take in, even to this very day.

She has come to realize that Jah delights in her happiness, but that is not His ultimate goal for her life. First, Jah's desire is that His kingdom be established on the earth (as it is in heaven)—that is, for His people to trust and obey Him completely, loving Him with all their hearts, minds, and strength. Second, He wants His will, His purpose to be accomplished by His people (just as with

His angels)—that is, for His people to share His love with those who do not yet know Him, and to love each other, loving their neighbors as themselves. As each person fulfills Jah's desires, they not only experience the temporal feeling of happiness, but also an everlasting joy that cannot be taken away. Jah takes delight in blessing those who trust and obey Him. One such special and most precious gift, she recognizes, came in the form of Cooran, her husband and best friend.

Sephina slightly tilts her head to look at her precious blessing and notices that Cooran seems to be caught up in deep thoughts himself. As they finish their tea, he takes her cup and puts them both to the side. He then wraps his blanketed arms around her, giving her a gentle squeeze, and kisses her on the lips. He comments on Jah's blessing in the beauty of the night's clear sky, starry heavens, and soft breezes. She nods and snuggles closer, rubbing his strong arms under the blanket and nestling her cheek against his. As they cuddle, they both drift back into silence.

Sephina's thoughts lead her to ponder some of her life's greatest and most valuable lessons. She discovered years ago that, no matter what challenges and destructive things the evil one may throw her way, he cannot take her life. However, that does not stop him from trying. The evil one understands that if anyone chooses to follow Jah, he, the evil one, has lost his ultimate goal to capture and destroy that person's spirit. The evil one desires to lead as many as possible to spend eternity with him in darkness, torment, and eternal death, forever separated from Jah. If he, the evil one, cannot do that, his aim is to deceive and cause many to disobey Jah and lose out on the earthly blessings and eternal rewards Jah has for them.

Even so, the evil one can never take away the eternal life of anyone whose god is Jah. That lesson alone was life changing for Sephina. To learn that to obtain eternal life comes only through a relationship with Jah is the simplest and greatest lesson ever. She is forever thankful that she, Cooran, Maneisha, Emily, their families, and many of their friends have all chosen Jah as their one true God.

Sephina knows and understands that when her time comes to leave this life on earth – her temporary home, who she really is—her spirit—will be eternally in Jah's loving presence. And there, she will reunite with her father and all those who trust and follow Jah, receiving

*The Ultimate Blessing—Eternity with Jah!*

# HEART OF THE KING

Jah is Love!
Jah loves me, so I must love myself.
I must love myself, in order to love Jah.
As a reflection of my love for Jah,
I must love my neighbors

as I love myself.

# NOTE FROM THE AUTHOR

Thank you for joining me on *The Sephina Series* adventure. I pray that you enjoyed reading it and hope you found some helpful life lessons along the way. My greatest desire though, is that it has inspired you to establish or to develop a deeper relationship with Jah (God). Either way, I would encourage you to pray the prayer below. If you already have a relationship with God—a bond, not just religion or ritual—then pray this prayer as a rededication of your commitment to Him, to grow closer, trusting, obeying, and totally relying on Him for your everything. If you have not yet invited God into your heart and received Him as Lord of your life, pray this prayer, believing in your heart by faith that you will receive the abundant life that only God has for you, the life that only your trusting in Jah can provide to you.

*Dear Father God,*

*I,_____, thank You for loving me so much that You sent Your Son, Jesus, to come to earth as a man: to live as an example for me to follow; to be beaten for my healing; and to shed His blood, dying on the cross and being buried so that my sins could be forgiven. Then You raised Him from the dead by the power of Your Holy Spirit, so that I can spend eternity (eternal life) with You.*

*Therefore, I confess unashamedly that Jesus Christ is my Savior, and I surrender all that I am, all that I possess, and all that I hope to become to Him as my Lord. I surrender my spirit, my soul, and my body to trust and obey You, Father God; following the leading of Your Holy Spirit, and to live under the truth of Your infalliable, holy, Word—the Bible. I also believe that because Jesus was resurrected from the dead—He is alive! By my faith in Him, Jesus now lives within my heart - exchanging my sin nature for His Christ-like nature. May You be glorified as I obediently trust Him to live in and through me. This I pray in Jesus' Holy Name. Thank You, Father!*

Now that you have prayed this prayer by faith, believing ... congratulations! If it is your first time, you have received the ultimate blessing: eternal life. Welcome into the awesome family of God. The angels in heaven are rejoicing. If you are rededicating your commitment to live for Christ, that is awesome! You are starting fresh, never to turn away again. In either case, you have now entered a new beginning, and your best days are before you. You will still experience life's ups and downs, but God will be with you every step of the way. Just keep your eyes and trust focused on Him. Also, please let me know through my website, www. thesephinaseries.com, that you did pray this prayer, so I can rejoice with you, Jah, and His angels.

I encourage you to obtain a Bible, with both Old and New Testaments, for your personal use. Read and study it daily. Stay consistent. Develop a regular quiet time, talking with the Lord. Start with as little as ten minutes a day. If you miss a day, just pick it up the following day. Study the entire book of Colossians, then, the books of St. John and Romans. Ask God to empower you with the Gift of His Holy Spirit. Allow the Holy Spirit to guide you as you read and to open your understanding of His Word. Also ask Him to guide you to a Bible-believing, faith-filled church, where you can learn, grow, and serve. Listen for His still, small voice for direction and guidance.

I am excited about your journey with God and the great plan He has for your life. Trust and obey Him. He loves you as no one else can. Don't forget to share God's love to and with others. Kind words and a smile can demolish some of the strongest walls and take down some of the biggest bullies. ☺ God's continuous *blessing* upon your life and that of your family. And I look forward to the day when you and I experience the Ultimate Blessing. Much love, from your new sister in Christ *Jesus*!

# JAH IS…

| Jah (God) is … | Bible is/tells of … | You are … |
|---|---|---|
| Love (Unconditional) | from< Love Letter >to | Loved by God |
| Truth | Truth | Not a mistake |
| Creator | Word of God | Created by God |
| One True and Living God | God's inspired Word, written by man | Created for God's delight and glory |
| a Triune Being | < Instruction Manual > | a Triune Being |
| • Father God<br>• Jesus (Son)<br>• Holy Spirit (Comforter and Guide) | • Old Covenant (Law)<br>• New Covenant (Grace & Liberty)<br>• Eternal | • Spirit (YOU)<br>• Soul (will, mind, intellect, emotions)<br>• Body (earth suit) |
| Omnipresent | Indestructible | an Eternal Being |
| Creator of only Good | <Goodness vs evil one | Made in God's image |
| Omnipotent | Powerful | You were … |
| Omniscient | Infallible | Born with sin nature |
| Merciful | < Character > | Shown mercy |
| Gracious | < Giving Grace to > | You can be/have … |
| Giving | <Jesus' Life for > | Born again |
| Forgiving | <Jesus' Sacrifice for > | Forgiven |
| Faithful | < Faithfulness to > | Christlike nature |
| Just | < Justice shown to > | Justified ~ (Just as if I (you) never sinned) |
| Kind | < Kindness to > | Kind to others/self |
| Righteous | < Righteousness to > | in Right standing before God |

| Holy | Holy | Holy in eyes of God |
|---|---|---|
| Jesus is ... | <WORD made flesh | Power in your words |
| God's Begotten Son | < John 1:1-14 > | Adopted by God |
| 100% God & 100% man | <OT ~ signs of coming, NT ~ birth, life, death, resurrection & return> | Have Eternal Life ~ RESURRECTED~ thru Jesus Christ |

# GOLDEN NUGGETS ~ WORDS OF LIFE, PART I

## (Life Confessions for Personal/Spiritual Growth)

- God is good, and God loves me! He will never abandon me.
- God is truth, and His love is unconditional and irrevocable.
- Truth can never be changed, even though facts can.
- Obedience requires trust; God is trustworthy!
- Obedience brings the blessing.
- I am blessed, in order to be a blessing to others.
- I should always have an attitude of gratitude.
- There is more to be thankful for than to complain about.
- What I believe (faith) should be evident in my words and actions.
- The Greater One (Jah) lives in me, therefore, I have the mind of Christ.
- Through Christ, I am able to do whatever I put my mind to.
- If it is important to me, it is important to God. (Nothing is too BIG or too SMALL in God's eyes.)
- God's kingdom come and His will be done, with or without me, but He desires that His will be done with, in, by, and through me.
- I am responsible to do what God calls me to do, no matter what others may think, feel, say, or do.
- If I make myself available (with faith, trust, and obedience) to God, He will provide me the ability and resources needed.
- When I do my part, I enable God to do His part.
- God will not force me to do His will, but He desires me to.

- Nothing is impossible or too hard for God to make happen.
- God is in control, but He requires my faith, words, and actions to activate His plan for my life.
- I cannot please God without exercising faith in His Word.
- Knowledge is of little use without wisdom and implementation.

# GOLDEN NUGGETS ~ WORDS OF LIFE, PART II

## (Life Confessions for Personal/Spiritual Growth)

"So then FAITH cometh by hearing, and hearing by the word of God" (Romans 10:17 KJV). Therefore, the more I hear and speak God's Word [when I speak, I hear it twice—both internally and externally], the stronger my FAITH becomes.

Right Hearing (Listening to God's Words) (leads to:) > Right Thinking (Thoughts/Visions/Dreams) > Right Believing (Faith) > Right Speaking (Words) > Right Actions (Deeds).

FAITH without Action is useless. ACTION without Faith is fruitless.

FAITH enables God to move in my life and on my behalf.

FEAR enables satan - the evil one - to wreak havoc in my life causing death and destruction. Therefore, I should always walk and speak in FAITH and never in FEAR.

FEAR is not from God. God gives me a spirit of POWER, LOVE and SELF-CONTROL (2 Timothy 1:7 ESV).

God does not want me to FEAR (be afraid of) Him, but, to REVERENCE (worship/adore/respect) Him, reflecting my TRUST / FAITH in Him.

FAITH is my confidence in the authority that God has given me through/by Jesus Christ (the WORD made flesh).

## (WHERE THERE IS AUTHORITY, THERE IS POWER)

Whether it be the AUTHORITY ...
>    ... of the Blood of Jesus Christ
>    ... in the Name of Jesus Christ
>    ... by the Word(s) of Jesus Christ
>    ... through the Person of Jesus Christ

My RIGHTEOUSNESS (right standing with God) in Christ Jesus, gives me ALL AUTHORITY.

AUTHORITY requires Responsibility; RESPONSIBILITY grants Authority.

You have authority for the words spoken over you. Do NOT allow what others think of, or say to or about you determine who you are. Use their destructive and constructive words to become the best You, you can be.

"Death and Life are in the power of *my* tongue" (Proverbs 18:21 KJV). Therefore, I must always speak WORDS OF LIFE over, in, and about my own and others' life, health, finances, and circumstances.

# GOLDEN NUGGETS ~ WORDS OF LIFE, PART III

## (Life Confessions for Personal/Spiritual Growth)

I must continuously speak what I want (contrary to any negative thoughts or feelings) in and by faith (believing), in order for it to come to pass (manifest). Again, I must be sure to speak *only* WORDS OF LIFE.

GOD's WORDS are TRUTH and LIFE. I will trust God's Words, not my circumstances or feelings. I should never react to my *circumstance(s)* or my feeling(s), but always act according to *GOD's Word*.

FORGIVENESS / LOVE: is a CHOICE.

It is just as important to RECEIVE *forgiveness/love* as it is to GIVE *forgiveness/love*.

It is just as important to *forgive/love* MYSELF as it is to *forgive/love* OTHERS.

Always be willing and ready to forgive, no matter the offense.

Strive to never take offense at what others may say or do.

The offender is not my enemy, but someone who allows satan to use them.

I will NOT allow satan to use me to offend or hurt others by words or deeds.

Satan always takes the TRUTH and twists
it for his destructive purposes.

Satan is a counterfeiter and the father of lies.
I will not listen to a word he says.

Satan will always make a situation seem worse than it really is.

Satan is an enemy that has already been
defeated. With Christ, I win!

No matter how big or bad the situation is, it
is NOT bigger than the God I serve.

Who / what God has BLESSED *cannot* be
cursed. ~ I am Blessed of the Lord!

The PEACE *of God* brings PROTECTION and
PROVISION for my family and me.

*God's* PROTECTION and PROVISION for my
family and me brings me PEACE.

Life on earth is temporary, yet I must be ALL
I can be ~ for my rewards are eternal.

Do NOT allow Disappointments to destroy, diminish,
or deter you from fulfilling your DREAM(S).

God is my SOURCE, and my job/career is only "a" Resource
God uses. I am NOT limited by my Resource(s), when
God, who is limitless, is my SOURCE. So I can dream
and *Dream BIG!—and even see those dreams fulfilled!*

*There is Hope in CHRIST JESUS!*

# ACKNOWLEDGMENTS

First, I'd like to thank God for the idea and inspiration for this book. As like King Rohaan, I am so blessed to have Jah entrust me with this, His plan, *The Sephina Series*. It started out to be a single Disney-like book, 16 pages at most plus illustrations, featuring what would have been the first Nubian Princess. So that tells you how long this book has been in the making. ☺ The first draft didn't even include a prince. Then God moved me to book two, then three, and eventually to the nine that have been combined as one. God made this a fun venture for me. He used this avenue to tame (not take away) my dreaming and wild imagination, to create something productive and meaningful. God truly has a great sense of humor. He is kind and He loves me. Thank You, Lord!

Second, I must thank my baby "titta", Tabatha, who has been a great inspiration. She is the illustrator of both Sephina and Cooran's characters and the designer of Sephina's coat; she was my sounding board for different aspects of *The Sephina Series*; she was my honest, constructive critic when critiquing my half-hearted, "rush-to-finish it all" at book four (some years ago); and she motivated me with her vivid imagination, drinking in my story, when she thought I was on the right track. Tab, TanQ!

Thanks to each of my sample readers: Cottrice Robinson, Gabriella Bowe, Charlotte Kay, Eric Schroeder, Mark Medina, Amy Moreno, Noella Smith, and Stern Ferguson. Each of you contributed useful feedback. Special thanks to Olivia Moore, who read the completed original and provided the back cover's Invitation to Readers. Thanks to Edwin and Anne-Marie Duboulay, as my unpaid editors.

Thanks to Carles Williams II and Donatha Bullard for your pointers for illustrations and self-publishing tips. Thanks to my "almost" illustrators: Raquel Ferguson and Amy Moreno for your valuable time and efforts. Thanks to my dad, Carles Williams, Aunt Maedon Roberts, many family members, my WOL family, and friends who encouraged my great undertaking, and especially those of you who supported by pre-buying. Thanks to Chester and Letty Rolle, whose devotion and love for God and each other reignited my passion, as a teen, back toward God. Many thanks to Aunt Evelena Beckham, other aunts, uncles, and others from my youth (many already passed on while few still remain) who prayed for and encouraged me in my walk with God. Thanks to friends like Kerlena Isaac, Tonya Lee, and Maxine Tucker for your fervent prayers that helped me through the final chapters to complete *The Sephina Series*. Special thanks to my artists, Alfrena Moosa and Tabatha Williams, you both beautifully fulfilled my illustration needs on short notice. Thanks to LeZette Knight for your computer-savvy assistance. Extra thanks to Michelle Maiden for thoroughly reviewing the revised version, you gave invaluable input. Final thanks to my mom, LaVerne Smith, as my beautician, you endured many hours of listening to me read and reread about Sephina, while you took care of my hair needs.

To my WestBow Press team, thanks in advance for making this project happen by bringing my baby, Sephina, to life. I am excited and looking forward to seeing the final outcome. Special thanks to Daniel P. and Paul H., my editors, for your priceless recommendations, creative ideas, and greatly needed grammatical assistance, all of which truly enhance this project. Thanks to Bob D. for your patience and to my production team for perfectly fulfilling my requests. Overflowing thanks to all!